Style and the Solitary

A Jerusalem Murder Mystery

Miriam Drori

Ocelot Press

Design: Services for Authors

First published in 2021 by darkstroke, Crooked Cat Books.
This revised edition published in 2022 by Miriam Drori in association with Ocelot Press.
Find Ocelot Press at **https://ocelot-press.com**
and Miriam Drori at **https://miriamdrori.com**

For my daughter, Aya Drori, talented singer and songwriter, who always asks about my books.

Acknowledgements

I am most grateful to the following for their help in crafting this novel: Melina Kantor, Shoshana Raun, Joan Livingston, and Stephanie Patterson (the brilliant editor). Also to Laurence Patterson for another beautiful cover.

I am also indebted to the late Gill Downs, without whom I wouldn't have become an author.

And a special 'thank you' to the authors at **Ocelot Press**, who welcomed me into their fold and provided much-needed support. More information about **Ocelot Press** can be found after the novel.

About the Author

Miriam Drori was born and brought up in the UK and now lives in Israel. While her stories are set mostly in those two countries, she has travelled widely and likes to feature exotic parts of the world, too.

Miriam has four published novels, so far, and one non-fiction book. A few of her short stories have also seen the light, the last being *Teamwork* in the *Dark Venice* charity anthology. She sees the recent acceptance of two poems for collections as a double fluke, as she is not a poet.

Miriam is passionate about raising awareness of social anxiety. It doesn't poke its ugly head into all her writing, but she's ready to deal with it when it does.

Style and the Solitary

A Jerusalem Murder Mystery

Foreword

Oh, the lessons we can learn from fairy tales. Such is the case of Beauty and the Beast, in which a young woman transforms a monstrous being into the prince he really is because she accepts him. That is what believing can do.

In her mystery, *Style and the Solitary*, author Miriam Drori brings that fairy tale to modern-day Jerusalem, where Asaf Levitt is misunderstood by his fellow workers and as the novel unfolds, by so many people. Who is this creature that at the book's start leaves home with a note in his pocket and a pledge that when he returns, "the deed would be done?" Could he be a beast capable of some awful deed, say murder, as the police later suspect?

In her previous two books, Miriam brought to the forefront how people can suffer terribly from social anxiety: the non-fiction book, *Social Anxiety Revealed*, and the novel, *Cultivating a Fuji*. She continued that exploration in *Style and the Solitary* when she created Asaf.

Those who have social anxiety are extremely ill at ease in public situations, and like Asaf, have a difficult time starting and maintaining a conversation. It is easy to see how so many could misinterpret such behavior and assume the person is hiding something. Truly, the only thing these sensitive people are hiding is themselves.

In Asaf's case, his social anxiety makes him vulnerable, certainly to the police who seek to quickly solve a murder. After all, he fits that classic profile of the loner who is quiet and keeps to himself. But there is more to Asaf than that, and fortunately a colleague recognizes this. Like the heroine in that fairy tale, Nathalie sees beyond his self-protective demeanor. Asaf is not a monster after all but someone worth knowing, and that's the key to solving his and the story's mystery.

Joan Livingston is the author of the Isabel Long Mystery Series, published by darkstroke books.

Chapter 1: Change is In the Air

Asaf Levitt pushed a hand into the arctic atmosphere outside the bedclothes and killed the music, dead. Instantly, he was up, throwing off the bedclothes and racing to complete the morning chores in record time. Washing, shaving, dressing, breakfast of cornflakes with milk, toast and cheese, apple juice. No need for a hot drink; that could wait for a break at the office. Bed-stripping and -folding to turn the bed into a sofa, washing up, because a tidy flat would welcome him back with open arms; a messy one would depress him, like a relationship gone sour – not that he knew anything about relationships.

Winter jacket with hood, gloves in pockets. Asaf gave his black shoes an extra little polish. Then he checked his image in the wardrobe mirror and felt around in his pockets. Keys, phone, wallet with cards and money. And the note, written last night, folded twice. He rubbed his thumb and forefinger against its smooth surface. The rubbing gave him courage, determination, like the touching of two wires to complete an electric circuit. Nothing would put him off, this time. Nothing and no one.

Asaf turned the key to unlock the front door, using his foot to push aside the draft stopper. When he returned, he would have done the deed and things would be different. Yes, people were about to take notice of him. Change was in the air.

The cold wind hit him as soon as he stepped out of the flat. This block didn't have an outside door, and living on the ground floor didn't help. Outside the building, the wind swirled around him. Asaf cut through it with hooded head lowered, as he charged ahead along almost-deserted pavements. He passed closed, lifeless shops. Even the grocer, though open for business, had its entrance closed to keep the weather out.

Other early birds waited at the bus stop on Hebron Road. Asaf recognised most of the faces and some of the voices. They probably recognised him. One thing he was sure of: none of them had ever heard his voice. He'd never approached them, and they usually left him alone. There was that time when a newcomer had asked him which bus he needed to get to the central bus station. He shrugged and raised his eyebrows, despite knowing the answer, and someone else offered the information.

The 71 turned up and most of those waiting crowded around the entrance. Asaf stood at the back, where no one would blame him for shoving them. There were generally enough seats, anyway, at this time. If not, standing was no hardship for him. As usual, he was the one to grant the card reading machine a minute or two of peace before the next lot of cards appeared.

This morning – was this a sign? – he even won a prize for being last on. A window seat, vacated when two people prepared to get off at the next stop. A chance to get up to date with news headlines on his phone, as well as to glance up at the familiar sites passing by. The Bank Junction, nicknamed after the numerous bank branches. Its name had stuck, although several of them had since changed identities. The streets of the neighbourhood of Baka on the left, then Abu Tor, the mixed Jewish and Arab neighbourhood, on the right. The First Station, once Jerusalem's railway station, now an outdoor cultural and culinary centre that hosted shows and boasted the start of a walking and cycling path leading as far as the zoo. Yemin Moshe, the beautiful old, road-free neighbourhood easily identifiable by its tall windmill. The town centre, and then the orthodox areas, noticeable especially by the dress of those traversing the streets, chatting together or scampering in all directions.

Perched on his window seat, Asaf took in all these sites, and skimmed the news on his phone, but still focused on his self-imposed mission for today. Nothing could stop him. Not after the events of Thursday, the last working day before the weekend. Thursday was a bad day, but sometimes you needed bad things to occur because they pushed you to break out of your comfort zone. Like the time he hit back at some twerp at school, who fell down in surprise, and for a change the laughter had diverted from Asaf to the twerp.

The screen on his phone turned itself off, but Asaf continued to stare at it.

Thursday. It was about eleven when he found out – after everyone else, naturally. He'd been concentrating on a particularly difficult circuit board, trying to work out the best components to fit into a tiny space, and he'd just had a lightbulb moment when Ido had put his black-haired head round the opening to Asaf's cubicle, all smiles and false friendliness. Typical. Ido always appeared at the worst moments and commanded attention solely by his presence.

Asaf should have told Ido to wait because he was busy. He should at least have said he needed another minute, so that he could write down his lightbulb thoughts before shifting his attention to Ido. But he didn't. He never did. The truth was – and this was hard to admit but had to be said – he was in awe of Ido.

Yes. Ido, who was hopeless at his job in quality assurance. Ido, who said, "Yes, of course I understand." Ido who came back to Asaf to ask yet again and feigned friendliness until Asaf had practically run the whole procedure himself, because there were only so many times you could explain the same thing.

"Asaf, you're a brick. I'm indebted to you. I'll tell Omer how helpful you've been to me."

Like hell you will, thought Asaf. You'll never tell the boss I did your work for you. You'll pretend it was all you, and he'll believe you because you could talk your way out of a snake pit. You could persuade a murderer to release you from the knife on your neck. And you know I won't tell Omer, despite being absolutely exasperated with you, because it would be too much of an effort for me to get the words out. Omer wouldn't believe me anyway. I know that and you know that. It's win-win for you and lose-lose for me. Every single bloody time.

Yes, this was that same Ido who Asaf was in awe of, precisely because of his ability to use his tongue to get everyone on his side.

But on Thursday, Ido hadn't come with any of his scribblings in hand or asked Asaf to review any of his measly attempts. No, Ido had come with an excited grin between his spiked hair and neatly trimmed beard, and a piece of news.

"Guess what. I've been promoted!"

"What!" Even Asaf couldn't keep quiet at that.

"I know; I was amazed, too. They think I'm ready to manage a team and, with Koby in the other office leaving, there's one going. Isn't that wonderful?"

"Yes. Congratulations." Asaf's reply was weak and emotionless, but that wouldn't raise any eyebrows. Asaf always sounded quiet and lacking in feelings.

"Cheers, mate." Ido thumped Asaf on the back. "I'm ordering cake for this afternoon. Two o'clock. Don't forget." Ido's actions were apparently friendly, but Asaf sensed the underlying scorn. What Ido was really saying was, 'Huh, you see? You sit here glued to your desk, slaving away at your simulated designs with their intricate components, but I'm the one who gets promoted. I'm the one who's going to get ahead in life. Ten years from now, I'll be a big boss over a whole department or a whole company. I'll have a large office all to myself, and you'll still be sitting in your little cubicle taking commands from up above.'

Asaf had lolled back in his chair after Ido left him. He'd been working at the office longer than Ido, he was far, far better at his work than him, and he would never be promoted. He would be shoved into a corner, consulted but never praised, all his life, unless he acted to stop that trend.

He hadn't forgotten the ideas of his lightbulb moment. They were all still there in his brain, and he knew that if he followed them, he would have his solution. But somehow, they didn't arouse the same excitement that he'd had before. The light wasn't as bright as it had been before Ido's rude interruption.

Asaf hadn't joined in the cake party. He'd remained in his cubicle, sitting on the little chair and laying his arms in front of the keyboard. He remembered resting his head on his arms and closing his eyes, hearing but not listening to the chatting from people who were, no doubt, pleased he hadn't turned up.

Although the content of their empty words passed him by, Asaf couldn't help picking out their voices, and marvelling at the way they all sounded so natural, so unlike him. Besides Ido, there was Omer, his team leader, and Gidon, the big boss, Sagi, the secretary, Kfir, Carmel and Reut. And Nathalie, whose very name could raise his spirits. She was different from the rest, French for a start, her cute accent and often quirky Hebrew bringing unexpected joy. And although she was lively and got on well with everyone, she either actually enjoyed talking to Asaf or she did a very good job of pretending to. Asaf couldn't make it out. Why would she want to be bothered with a beast like him? Yet, over the three months since Nathalie had joined the team, Asaf had found himself increasingly looking forward to the times he and Nathalie worked together.

While the little party endured, while Asaf heard but didn't listen, the seed of his idea planted itself in his brain. And he knew he had to put it into action whatever the consequences. Even if it meant never seeing Nathalie again. During the weekend, he thought of nothing else.

Now, on the bus, he hummed two songs to himself, both called *Today*. He picked out the lines that meant the most to him, the ones that looked forward to this day which was just beginning, and which would be the start of something new, something good, something unusual.

Quicker than ever, yet at the usual time, the bus stopped by the Har Hotzvim Technological Park. Asaf, standing ready by the door, hands in pockets, fingers rubbing the folded note, stepped down to the outside and began the brisk five-minute walk to the office, past the roar of drilling from the building site of yet another office block. Today, the strong, icy wind pushed him on, whispering in his ears, "Go. Reach the office as usual, but be ready for this to be an extraordinary day. A most extraordinary day." His heart thumping against its walls, Asaf punched in the code and pushed open the door to his block, confident that he understood this message, that he had the situation under control, that every extraordinary thing that would happen on this day depended on him making the first move.

"Morning," Asaf called to the guard before hurrying on towards the lifts, the guard's fading reply echoing in his ears.

It had become Asaf's job to be the first to arrive at the office. Nearly every morning, he'd unlock the door, and then rush to turn off the alarm before it screeched its ugly noise and notified the security company.

Inside the lift, his jacket now hooked in his arm, he pressed the button marked **3** and checked his appearance in the mirror while being transported to the place that had been his second home for three long years. A short walk brought him to the heavy door. He reached into his pocket and brought out the bunch of keys, chose one and pushed it into the lock.

He was ready.

Chapter 2: La Belle

"*Oh là là!*"

Nathalie Weyl raised her whole body to sit bolt upright. Images still flew in front of her eyes. Gory images with distorted faces and the bright red of blood, along with excruciating sounds of screaming and thunder, and scary flashes of lightning. She rubbed her eyes in an attempt to expunge them, but still they lingered, especially the changing face of the body at the end. "*Mon Dieu!*" It was awful, the way it kept morphing from one face to another. At one point, it was a donkey as in the illustration by Warwick Goble. Then it was a human, scarred face, then a leering face surrounded by long, straggly grey hair, then someone she recognised. With a gasp, she realised the last face belonged to Asaf. Perhaps this dream was telling her something… Something she had to do to help him. Because it couldn't mean Asaf was going to be a murder victim. That would be too terrible.

Taking deep breaths to calm herself, Nathalie waited until her heartbeat slowed to a normal pace. She looked around the room, dimly lit by the lights outside. Everything looked so normal. How strange that this happened. She wasn't prone to nightmares at all, and certainly not to such violent and messy ones. What could have caused this?

Putting on the silky silvery grey dressing gown that matched her pyjamas, and warm, furry slippers, she made her way to the kitchen, encountering only reassuring normality, and made herself a mug of tea, which she carefully carried back to her bedside table. "*C'est mieux,*" she murmured between sips of the soothing beverage. *That's better.*

She shook her head, still perplexed by the nightmare. True, last night, just before going to bed, she'd told Tehila all about *Beauty and the Beast*, surprising her flatmate, who thought the story was a children's fairy tale. "No." Nathalie had hastened to put her friend right. "*Beauty and the Beast* was written long before the Disney Company turned it into a cartoon. The original story was written by a woman called Gabrielle-Suzanne Barbot de Villeneuve in 1740."

"1740, and a woman! That's amazing," said Tehila.

"She was very rich and had a lot of influence. Actually, she lost her wealth but still had influence. She wrote the story to teach people a lesson."

"What lesson?"

"At the end of the story, Beauty searches for the Beast and finds he has been murdered. She is so sad, and she screams, 'I am sorry! This was all my fault!' When she says that, the Beast turns into a handsome prince. And the lesson is that when someone believes in you, you can become a different person, or the person you were meant to be."

Tehila nodded slowly. "How do you know all about this?"

"You forget that I studied French Literature at the Sorbonne."

"All that studying, and you didn't even use it. You went into something completely different."

"Everything you learn is useful and can affect you in some way. When you learn it, you can't possibly know how it will be useful to you in the future. One day, we might even find a use for differential equations."

Tehila sniggered. "I'd have to relearn them, first. But it's true what you say. I don't work in hairdressing any more, but it's a skill I use on my own hair, and it might well have other uses at other points in my life."

Nathalie had looked up at Tehila's hair, naturally fuzzy, black and very curly. Yesterday, it was tied into long braids. Other times, it was gathered up into a knot above her head, or hanging loose. She'd seen Tehila working on her hair and felt secretly thankful that hers was basically straight and easy to manage.

Setting down her teacup, Nathalie again shook her head. Last night's talk of that violent story didn't explain the ferocity of the nightmare, or any nightmare at all. It was so unlike her to be affected in that way.

Nathalie slid down, revelling in the warmth of her duvet, and wiggled her feet under the extra blanket, which helped to keep her feet from freezing over. Scared that sleep would bring another nightmare, she remained awake, but now calm and serene. Moving to another country was never going to be easy, and Israel wasn't the easiest of countries to choose. Yet, there had been a weird sense of belonging to this place from the beginning. The language had been hard to acquire and she still struggled with it sometimes. Some of the other French immigrants she'd met spoke fluent Hebrew, having learnt the language as children. They mostly came from Paris. In Strasbourg, Jews didn't normally learn Hebrew, and her parents had never seen a need for it.

However, Nathalie was lucky with her chosen profession. Leaving the Sorbonne with a degree in French Literature, unsure how to proceed, she came across a course in PCB layout design. She didn't even know what PCB stood for. The words 'printed circuit board' only brought up a mental image of a small green metal board with lots of funny little shapes attached, and lines all over the place. Rather like an aerial urban street map.

She had almost ignored the flyer, but paused at the list of qualities required: attention to detail, interest in technology, ability to solve problems and social aptitude. She liked the sound of that mixture and went for the course. Her PCB design certificate and two years of experience had served her much better in Israel than all her knowledge of French and its literature. But, as she'd told Tehila yesterday, you never knew when and how stuff you learned could be useful.

Memories of telling Tehila about *Beauty and the Beast* led back to that strange and frightening dream. And to Asaf. She saw his sweet, blue-eyed, babyish face, with mousy hair combed to one side and a rounded, slightly protruding chin. It was incongruous in the violent dream, amongst the other, scary faces.

Asaf was different from all the others in the office, like Gidon, Omer, Sagi, Ido, Kfir, Carmel and Reut. They were all loud, friendly, no-nonsense people. Yes, like typical Israelis, they gave you their thoughts with no wrapping. *Dugri*. She'd internalised this slang word for straight talking. But Asaf kept his thoughts bottled up. The others assumed he didn't have any, but she was sure they were wrong. His face showed it.

Did the dream mean that Asaf needed her help? She was already doing her best to draw him out, proud of her tiny 'wins'. But if the dream was trying to tell her anything at all, it was that she should do a lot more. What else could she do?

She'd yearned to bore inside Asaf's head from the beginning, when she first started working in the office. He was clearly intelligent, yet so closed up, almost as if he felt he had to hide who he was. Nathalie had felt frustrated at first, because nothing she tried ever worked. She remembered that Saturday morning when everything was new – her work, the apartment and her roommates. She must have got out of bed on the wrong side, that morning. Everything aggravated her, starting with a steadily worsening headache.

She knew what would ease the pain and marched straight to the kitchen, in her nightgown, to get it. There, she found Yarden cuddling a steaming mug, curly locks flopping with untidy stubbornness over her face.

Nathalie opened a cupboard. “Where’s the coffee?”

“I just finished it.” Yarden didn’t even sound guilty. She continued to sip the last of the coveted drink, while Nathalie watched, and she didn’t bat an eyelid.

“Wasn’t it your turn to buy more?”

“It was, but I didn’t. It slipped my mind. Sorry.”

“Yarden, my head’s killing me and I need coffee. What are you going to do about it?”

“Well, I can hardly go out and buy some on a Saturday. There’s some Acamol in the bathroom.”

Nathalie shook her head and sulked. Why would she take a pill when all she needed was caffeine?

“Tell me, Nathalie. Is that really what’s got into you, this morning, or are you picking on me because there’s something bigger going on?” Yarden flicked the curls away from her eyes for the umpteenth time.

“I really am upset with you for not doing your chores, but it’s true there’s something else going on.”

“Care to tell me what that is?”

“All right. I’ll just make myself a cup of tea first.” She emphasized the word ‘tea’, glaring at Yarden. Then, though not entirely happy with the response, she got busy preparing it.

Sitting at the little table opposite her still-new flatmate, having imbibed a few sips of calming tea, Nathalie explained. “There’s a guy called Asaf at work. Actually, there are a few nice guys at work who are probably still single, but Asaf is special and different.”

“But he doesn’t like you?”

“I don’t know what he likes. He’s a closed book, to everyone. I’ve tried different ways to draw him out, but he doesn’t take the bait.”

Yarden sighed. "How did I guess this would be about love? You French people – that's all you think about, isn't it? Listen, if he's not interested, then leave him alone. Try one of the others, if you must. You have time. Twenty-four isn't quite over the hill, you know."

Nathalie didn't react to the second part of that, because the first part made her arms wave even before Yarden had finished. "Israelis talk about love at least as much as French people, but I don't say all Israelis think about is love. You also talk about the weather a lot, but no one says Israelis only think about the weather. You leave that for the British. People are people, wherever they come from. Everyone is unique. The British can fall in love, the French can discuss the weather and Israelis can stop winding people up – if they try especially hard."

Yarden had the chutzpah to smirk. "I think you've wound yourself up."

Now, still lying in bed, Nathalie again shook her head. Yarden didn't understand. Nathalie couldn't possibly have taken her advice to forget about Asaf, because her intuition told her something else. She continued to try with him whenever opportunities arose, and now felt the tide was gradually turning. But it was still a hard slog – no walk in the park. Oh dear, what a mix of metaphors. But yes, three months in, she was only now beginning to solve the riddle that was Asaf.

The sound of movement outside her room woke Nathalie to the start of a new day: Sunday. That was another facet of Israeli life that took a lot of getting used to. Her brain still told her that working on a Sunday was wrong. Sunday was a day for relaxing or for getting out and doing things that were different to what she did on other days. Sunday was also a day for hearing the sweet ring of church bells and remembering she was different.

The dull grey showing through the curtain on this Sunday didn't galvanise her to begin her day, but she dutifully took her turn in the bathroom and returned to dress and put on makeup.

'Enough but not too much.' Her mother's wise words always echoed during this process.

Then she emerged to the mess that was the kitchen. She sighed. Tehila wasn't too bad, but Yarden was something else, never seeing the problem of dirty dishes piled high in the sink. But this wasn't the first time Nathalie had shared an apartment, and she knew better than to try to impose her own strict standards. Yarden was a good friend and Nathalie wanted their friendship to continue. Fortunately, an almost-full jar of coffee greeted her from the cupboard.

Nathalie put a frozen croissant in the microwave and flicked the switch on the warm kettle for her morning drink.

"Good morning." Yarden, in her dressing gown, started to prepare her own breakfast. "Wish me luck."

"Luck? What for?"

"I have three days to finish my project and I haven't even started it."

"When were you given the assignment?"

"About two months ago."

"So, why…?"

"Yeah, I know. I kept putting it off."

Nathalie shook her head and opened the palms of her hands. "When will you learn?"

"Nathalie, some people are organised like you; others live from one crisis to the next. And I happen to belong to the group of others."

"No. Anyone can change the way they are. You just need confidence in yourself. You can do it."

"Okay, I'll try to start earlier next time. Right now, I'm in crisis mode."

"Good luck."

Nathalie finished off her coffee and croissant. Not as tasty as the fresh croissants she consumed in France, but a decent substitute she put up with in her new life. It wasn't that she couldn't buy fresh croissants here, but the early start left her no time for such luxuries.

Nathalie stamped her feet as she waited for the bus on the noisy Hebron Road. She was glad she'd wrapped up warmly, decked out in coat, boots, gloves and hat. She'd never expected Jerusalem to get so cold. Wasn't the Middle East supposed to be hot? In the office, there had even been talk of snow. Apparently, that could close the whole city down for a day, sometimes more.

Waiting with her was a group of schoolchildren, babbling away in excited tones. Kids were the hardest to follow. She was glad she hadn't gone into teaching. She'd considered it, before discovering PCB layout design, because there didn't seem many options with a French degree, although she wasn't looking forward to controlling large classes of bored kids. These children at the bus stop would be hell to teach. She imagined them mocking her accent with words she didn't even understand. No, hi-tech beat school hands down. Even the pay compared favourably.

The 71 bus arrived. Nathalie boarded, used her card, and found a seat at the back. The bus stop names flashed up on the screen and boomed out from the loudspeaker, but Nathalie no longer needed them.

She'd been lucky to be taken on by Gidel Electronics when fresh from ulpan with very flawed Hebrew. Gidel was a great place to work. The people were really friendly. They messed her around, sometimes, over her Hebrew bloopers and ignorance of Israeli culture, but they did it in a friendly way and also helped her to become acclimatised. The ulpan had been good for learning Hebrew, too, but it didn't give her a lot of practice with Israelis. In the three months she'd been working at Gidel, she'd become much more confident at talking.

As far as the work went, the person she had to interact with the most was Asaf. He was the one who designed the boards before she could do the layout. Asaf stuck out by not sticking out. He kept to himself, and she usually saw him alone in his cubicle, bent over his desk, either staring at intricate diagrams on a screen or using tweezers to move tiny components on a board, a magnifying glass attached to his head like an earphone headset. She'd see various instruments around him, like an oscilloscope, a voltmeter and a soldering iron, and he always seemed completely immersed in what he was doing. Even on Thursday, he didn't attend Ido's little party to celebrate his promotion.

Nathalie remembered her shock at the large piece of cream cake that Ido dumped on her plate. She remembered using her plastic fork to cut it into two, transferring the larger piece back to the central dish. She remembered taking tiny bites to make her piece last, and chatting with the others, still marvelling at the ease at which she did so. And all the while, she wondered about Asaf's absence. Did he mind that Ido had been promoted, or did he simply prefer to be alone? It was hard to know what went on behind his generally bland façade.

But she was working on it.

When they'd started working together, Asaf had seemed shy and hesitant, unsure of his ability to guide Nathalie. Yet he explained everything well. He was clearly very knowledgeable. It all seemed to come to him effortlessly, and yet he didn't assume it would be so easy for Nathalie. Not once did he imply that something was trivial and she should have understood it immediately.

Lately, they'd been having their coffee together and discussing other things – books, mostly. Nathalie had been impressed with Asaf's depth of reading, especially for an engineer. "Books have always been my escape from the real world," Asaf had ventured. "Mine, too," Nathalie had replied, feeling an unfamiliar warmth spreading through her body as he smiled and she returned in kind. She put this down to feelings that, at last, she was beginning to find a breach in the wall of his fortress.

The Har Hotzvim bus stop saw a mass exodus, as usual. Nathalie stood up from her seat at the back of the bus in the corner and followed the crowd to the exit. From there, a short walk took her to the tall office block that housed Gidel. The cold wind pushed her along, past the roar of drilling, as if impatient for her to reach the office. What's the hurry? she wondered, pushing up her coat sleeve with a gloved hand to make sure she wasn't late. Inside, Nathalie smiled to the guard, who recognised her now. They'd even enjoyed a couple of quick chats together. Today, he nodded but didn't smile, a faraway glaze to his eyes, and Nathalie made a mental note to ask after his father on the way out. She took the lift to the third floor, checking her face in the mirror on the way up.

The first sign that something was different was at the heavy door. Her card didn't open it. Was her card at fault, or was it the reader? Or had the door been locked, overriding the reader? How odd. Nathalie reached up and pressed the bell. She gasped when the door was opened immediately by a uniformed police officer.

Chapter 3: Occurrence in the Office

Although shocked by the turn of events, Nathalie's mind was still able to reason. The police officer, she decided, must have come from one of two dark blue police cars stopped on the road outside and blocking some of the parked vehicles, although when she'd arrived at the building, she hadn't really registered the police cars.

"Do you work here?" the officer asked. She was taller than Nathalie and her stern expression added to Nathalie's confusion.

"Yes." Nathalie hesitated, wondering what could have happened. A burglary, maybe?

"Please come in and go to sit with the others in the conference room."

A screen blocked the way forwards into the lobby, and the officer pointed to Nathalie's right, around the edge of the lobby.

The conference room was at the end of the corridor next to the one with the printer. As Nathalie passed the printer room, she saw a strange sight out of the corner of her eye, through the open door. At least, she thought she saw it. Surely, she was mistaken. Lack of sleep, the shock of being greeted by the police, and the infinitesimal amount of time available for the corner of her eye to process the sight must have all combined to confuse her brain.

In the conference room, most of the other workers were seated around the large oval-shaped table, staring into space. An eerie silence hung over them, most unusual for this group. What could have happened? Clearly, this was no time to ask. Nathalie hung her coat on the back of an empty chair and sat down to wait in the expectant gloom.

Six others sat at the table: Gidon, Omer, Sagi, Kfir, Carmel and Reut. Four people were missing. One, Nathalie remembered, was sick yesterday and another had taken a few days off. That left Ido and Asaf. A female police officer stood straight and still at the back, her face expressionless. Muffled sounds came from outside the room. Short, sharp sentences. Instructions. Inside, complete silence. Hardly a movement. Nathalie tried to concentrate on breathing. What she thought she had seen in that split second couldn't have been. It simply couldn't. But if it wasn't, then where was Asaf? More sounds reached her from outside. Squeaking, scraping. What was going on?

Time hung in the conference room.

Eventually, a man came in. Medium-height, strong build, grey and balding; in police uniform of navy-blue trousers and light blue shirt. Three silver-coloured diamond shapes sat on his shoulder. He owned them in his stride, in his countenance, in his command of presence.

Seven pairs of eyes watched him march straight to the vacant chair at the head of the table, sit down and speak. Clearly, he had no time to spare.

"Right. I'm Chief Inspector Barak Elad and I'm leading this investigation. I'm going to tell you what's happened. Then I'm going to interview each of you in turn and take statements, which may be used in court."

All heads were turned towards the chief inspector, as if commanded to do so. The expression on his face showed determination and dedication to the task at hand. Also, a sort of tiredness. He'd probably been through this scenario or one like it many times before.

"One of the employees in your office was found dead, probably murdered, early this morning in your lobby. His name is Ido Bitton."

A collective, sharp intake of breath could be heard.

"Another employee was found with a possible weapon in his hand and has been taken into custody to be arrested. His name is Asaf Levitt."

Another intake of breath. Someone didn't join in. When she'd recovered slightly from the initial shock, Nathalie realised that Omer, who was sitting next to her, remained perfectly still and quiet. In fact, he was leaning back in his chair, his long legs stretched out under the table, looking much more at ease than the rest. What could that mean? Did he already know what happened? How?

On the other side, across the wide, long table, Sagi began to sob. Did she know more? Sagi fished a tissue out of her bag. Carmel, who sat beside her, reached a tentative hand to her shoulder, but kept facing the chief inspector.

"No one may leave this room until the interviews are finished. In the meantime, these two officers…" as if on cue, two uniformed officers entered the room "…will take your fingerprints and DNA. This is a procedure required by law. You can't refuse it. Right, I'll start with…" he consulted a piece of paper in his hand "… Mr Gidon Regev. I understand you're the manager here?"

"Yes." Gidon stood up and followed the chief inspector out of the room. Despite the severity of the situation, Gidon's stride and the position of his head broadcast a sense of authority.

The two officers performed their duty quietly and efficiently, and Nathalie had time to think. She knew all these people around the table. She'd worked with them, chatted with them, laughed with them. She couldn't imagine any of them committing this terrible crime. Yet, without a doubt, Ido was dead and someone must have killed him. Who? How? And why?

The questions gave way to a sickening awakening. This was serious. Very serious. More serious than anything she'd experienced in her whole life. Nathalie felt a weight descending on her shoulders, an ache rising in her head. Her present and her future had suddenly become very fuzzy. She had no idea what the next minute would bring, let alone any later time. Of one thing, and one thing only, was she sure: Asaf couldn't be the murderer. She had to tell that to the chief inspector. What was his name? Barak Elad. Yes, that was the only thing that was clear in this awful mess. They'd made a big mistake arresting Asaf. She had to make sure he understood that.

So, that image caught by the corner of her eye had been correct. Asaf sitting on a chair in the printer room, handcuffed to a police officer. Nathalie would never forget the look on his pallid face, staring. He often looked afraid, but this was much more than usual. He was deadly frightened, and her heart went out to him. She had to help him because he was innocent, because he wouldn't help himself, and because he was a good person and she liked him a lot.

After some time, Gidon returned and Omer was called out. Then Kfir, Sagi, Carmel and Reut. Each of them was away for what seemed like an awfully long time, although not once did Nathalie check that impression against her watch. She felt scared of doing anything at all, as if the slightest movement could incriminate her in this terrible crime. Even thinking felt wrong, although she doubted the officers had taken a course in mindreading.

Sagi started to sob again after she returned to her seat and while Carmel was out of the room. Kfir, who was sitting on Sagi's other side, comforted her with an arm around her shoulder and a whisper. Sagi gave him a weak smile and blushed. Nathalie had the impression that the two shared some sort of secret. All sounds dissolved long before Carmel returned and Reut left.

Reut broke through the wall of silence and returned to her chair, as all the others had done. Then it was Nathalie's turn. She followed the female police officer to Gidon's expansive office. On the way, she couldn't help noticing the screen, again, hiding the centre of the lobby. That had to be where the body was, unless they'd taken it away already. That scraping sound… Were they scraping blood from the floor? Bile rose in her throat. She didn't want to see behind that screen.

"Have a seat, Nathalie."

She sat down opposite the chief inspector with his three diamond shapes. She pursed her lips, shrank into herself and looked up at him across the large desk. Then she remembered she had an important message to impart and puffed out her chest to give herself confidence.

On the desk were two piles of papers, one on each side, probably Gidon's, and a notepad on which Barak scribbled.

"How long have you worked here?"

"About three months." Did her newness in the company make her a suspect? "I'm a new immigrant," she explained. "From France."

He grinned, as if to say that's so obvious it's hardly worth mentioning. "Where do you live?"

"In the German Colony. I share an apartment with two other girls."

"Who are they?"

"Yarden is studying criminology and Tehila is studying acting."

"Tell me about your work, here."

"I'm a layout designer of printed circuit boards. I get the circuit design from engineering, along with a diagram of the functionality of the circuit. I do the artwork that's necessary to turn that into a printed circuit board. Then I have to hand everything over to manufacturing, which is done by an outside company."

"I see." He looked as though he didn't see. Nathalie wondered whether she'd said too much. But surely what she said showed that she knew her job, which had to be a good thing. At least, she thought so. Barak continued. "Who do you work with most closely in this company?"

"Asaf."

"How do you two get on together?"

"Very well. He's always helpful and patient. With his help, I soon picked up the way this company works and what it's trying to do. I enjoy being here."

"What about outside the actual work? Is Asaf easy to get on with?"

Nathalie thought for a moment. She suddenly felt as if her answer could make all the difference. "Asaf is quiet and shy. He seems to be really unsure of himself in social situations. It took a long time before he talked about anything outside our jobs. I had to work on it."

"Why?"

"I told you. Because he's so quiet. Maybe he thought I wouldn't be interested in what he does in his free time."

"No. Why did you bother to work on your relationship with Asaf?"

"Oh, I see. It seemed the natural thing to do. I had a roommate like that in my first year at university. She... I couldn't get through to her at the beginning. She'd answer my questions with one-word answers. By the end of the year, she was a different person. I'm sure I helped to make that change."

"And now you want to do the same with Asaf."

"Barak," she began. In her short time in this country, she'd learnt that first names worked where they didn't in France. She'd found using them helped her to level the playing field. Instead of being a subordinate looking up to a boss, she became a person talking to another person. Or, in this case, it lowered the chief inspector to the status of human being. "Barak, I'm not a psychologist and I'm not here to change anyone. But when I see someone who struggles with something, I try to help them. That's all."

"What does Asaf struggle with?"

"Well, these are just my thoughts…"

"Go on." He leaned forward.

"From the expressions on his face, I think he makes himself unhappy when he fails to express himself properly, and other people make him unhappy when they laugh at him. I mean, they don't laugh out loud – just a bit, to themselves."

Barak scribbled something before continuing. "What did you and Asaf talk about, then?"

"Books mostly."

"Books?"

"Yes, he's very well read for an engineer. He said that's because he has a lot of time to read. If you want to know what Asaf's like, I think that remark says a lot about his character. I tried to praise him, and he gave excuses, as if he had to show me he's not as good as I thought. It shows humility and a lack of confidence, in my opinion."

"Which types of books does he like?"

"Oh, various types. Even big classics like *War and Peace*."

"Did he ever talk about revenge?"

"Revenge?"

"Doing harm to someone else because they did something bad to him."

"Ah, *vengeance*. No, never."

Barak leaned forwards, resting his arms on Gidon's desk, and gave Nathalie a long, hard look. "Nathalie, my impression is that you've got to know Asaf better in three months than everyone else here has in three years."

Nathalie nodded. "You could be right. *My* impression is that the others cause Asaf to hide within himself. They make him feel worthless even though he has a lot to offer. Whereas I'm new and not very high up in the hierarchy. And I have my own struggles, with the language and being in a different country. I'll never pose any threat to him, so it's easier for him to relate to me."

"I want you to think carefully before you answer this question." Barak's face looked darker, and his eyes bore into her. "Do you think Asaf could be a murderer?"

Nathalie shook her head but took a moment before replying. After all, Barak had told her to think carefully. "No. Not at all. I don't think there's a trace of..." Nathalie held her clenched fists in a boxing position as she tried to remember the word.

"Violence?"

"...violence in him. He's a gentle, caring person. I think there's been a terrible mistake and it must be put right as soon as possible."

Worry lines appeared on Barak's forehead as he seemed to reflect on Nathalie's words. Then he reached for a form from a pile on top of one of Gidon's piles and picked up a pen. "Now, for the statement, could you just describe your movements this morning up to the moment you arrived at the office?"

***

The bus journey home felt years away from the one Nathalie had taken just a few hours before in the opposite direction. As the bus turned this way and that, her world suddenly took on a surreal quality. As if she no longer knew where it was going. In the nine months since she'd left home, she'd managed to take control of things. Her life had followed the route she'd planned for it: ulpan to learn Hebrew, a room to rent, a job, hopes that romance would come her way. Now, this thing had happened, and control was slipping away. The one person she might have had feelings for, out of those she'd met so far, had been locked up, accused of killing someone. It was unbelievable. This poor, sweet, gentle man had been taken away, suspected of having committed a heinous crime, and there was nothing she could do about it.

Or was there?

Chapter 4: Locked Inside

A visitor would have taken in the rough surfaces of the floor and walls, the two metal-framed beds, two plain wooden chairs and the high window protected by metal bars, and might well have labelled the place stark and uninviting. The mixture of smells, including damp and possibly sewage, would have added to the impression. The visitor would have seen the two men, sitting as far away from each other as possible in the small area. Even after being informed of the closeness of their ages, the visitor would have been more aware of the differences between these men than any similarities.

One – large, burly and unshaven, his muscly, bare arms covered with tattoos – was sitting on a bed and lolling back against the wall. He looked somehow at home in this place, or at least as if he knew it well.

The other sat in the corner of the hard stone floor, his head between raised knees. Draped over him was a coarse black blanket. He could have been mistaken for a pile of bedding if not for a couple of things. One was the pair of polished black shoes that showed beneath the blanket – shoes that looked too smart for this place. The other was the fact that the blanket and everything underneath it were shivering, although it wasn't particularly cold in here.

The visitor might have wondered about all these signs and what they could mean. But there was no visitor. There was never a visitor in this cell, only suspected criminals and their jailers. The criminals had other things on their minds and so did the jailers. Besides, they'd seen it all before, or they thought they had.

"Your first time, is it?"

The gruff voice caused the blanketed bundle to shudder. A head raised up from between the knees and the blanket moved to the side just enough for a pair of eyes to peep round it.

"I asked you a question. Is it your first time?"

The head nodded.

"What did you do?"

The head shook.

"I said, 'What did you do?'"

Finally, a voice came from behind the blanket – quiet, meek and high-pitched. "I didn't do it."

"Ha! You really are green, aren't you? They brought you here cos they think you're guilty. They're not going to take that."

"But it's the truth," wailed Blanket Man.

Tattoo Man roared with laughter. "The truth. Them up there…" He looked up towards the heavens. Or to the floor above. "…they're not interested in the fucking truth. All they want is to get you convicted and earn their fucking keep."

The eyes over the blanket opened wider.

"Take my advice," said Tattoo Man. "Tell them you're guilty and you'll get a lower sentence. What did you do, anyway?"

"They think I killed someone, but I didn't."

"Murder, that's a serious crime. A very serious crime. You wanna watch yourself."

"I didn't do it."

"Tell that to the judge."

Blanket Man gasped and put his head down again. The imaginary visitor might have been reminded of an ostrich.

"Wanna know what I did?" The gruff voice again.

The head came up for another nod.

"Robbery with violence, they call it. No violence needed, the old woman was so weak. All I had to do was pull her to a chair and tie her up."

Blanket Man shivered again.

A few minutes later, a key turned in the lock of the cell door and another big man called a name.

Blanket Man turned to look at the jailer.

"Come on, you dimwit. When I call your name, you stand up and come with me."

Blanket Man stood up and went to the gate. The jailer shook his head. "Now I've seen it all. Put that down on your bed. It's meant to keep you warm at night. It's not a bloody baby's security blanket."

The tattooed robber let out a loud, raucous laugh. Blanket Man blushed as he followed the instructions.

"Now walk that way." The jailer pointed along the corridor while locking the gate. "Faster! I ain't got all day."

***

"Hello, love," Chief Inspector Barak Elad said to the phone in his hand. "Look, I'm really sorry… Yeah, I know, but something came up… Shira, believe me, I wish I could. But this one's serious. Look, if you can do all the packing, I'll try to get back in time, but I can't promise… Yeah, I'll do my best."

Barak returned the phone to its holder a little too hard and spoke to the woman at the other desk. Rachel Paran. "She's fed up. I don't blame her. I promise her a holiday and then I tell her I don't know if I'll be able to make it. And it's not as if it's the first time. Honestly, I don't know why she stays with me, but she does."

"You're lucky. But she's lucky, too. She knows you do what you can."

"Haven't you ever wanted to settle down with someone?"

"I'm married to my job. I don't think I'm cut out for bigamy."

Barak shrugged, scrutinising his colleague. Short hair, never painted her nails or dressed up – not even for parties. Always in straight trousers and flat shoes, even when that wasn't uniform. Very good at her job, yes. But she missed that extra something, that umph that made a good detective excellent. Being married to the job was probably the reason. She didn't easily take on other personas when necessary. Too much the professional police officer.

For Barak, there was room for both in his life – his wife and family, and his job. Emotionally, physically, neither could be fully satisfying without the other. But one part of family life was impossible: making plans. Everything he did with Shira had to be spontaneous. That's what got her down. It wasn't fair on her. He would make it up to her. Definitely, absolutely, no question about it. He loved his wife even more than his job.

"Eilat, wasn't it?"

Barak nodded. "Sea, sun, beach, luxury hotel, vibrant nightlife. And snorkelling. We were both looking forward to that. We just wanted a week away from all the tension. Is that too much to ask?"

"Why don't you let me handle the case?" asked Rachel.

"I don't know. This is a murder. I'll tell you what. If I can get him to admit it all now, it should go smoothly after that. Then I'll leave it to you."

"I hope it works out."

A message buzzed through. "Prisoner ready and waiting."

Barak stood up. "Wish me luck." He placed his lips around an imaginary snorkel and made swimming movements with his arms on his way to the door.

Half an hour later, Barak stormed into the office, slamming the door behind him, and slumped down on his chair.

"That bad?" asked Rachel.

"He wouldn't talk." Barak groaned. "I tried everything. I cajoled him. I threatened him. I ended up shouting at him, I was so frustrated. He simply wouldn't talk."

"How d'you mean? You asked him questions and he said, 'No comment'?"

Barak shook his head. "I wish. He didn't say a word. Not one measly little word. Not even a sound. In all my forty years in the force, I've never known a prisoner to keep mum."

"But surely he had to talk to ask for legal aid."

"I even told him that. I told him it was in his interest to ask for legal aid. He just sat there staring at me. I told him I could phone his parents for him. Nothing. It was unnerving, I can tell you."

"How are you going to get him to talk?"

Barak closed his eyes for a moment, then looked back at Rachel. "I don't know."

"How about calling in the psychological unit?"

"The psychos? Not once in all the time I've worked in CID have I ever called in the psychos. What can they know about people that I haven't picked up on my own?"

"They might know how to make your dumbo talk."

"I don't believe it. All they do is to talk a lot of twaddle. They'll probably come up with some story. How he visited his dad in prison and now he has a phobia of prisons. You know the sort of thing. What help is that in a murder trial? No, mark my words: I'll never call in the psychos."

She arrived full of youthful pomposity, head held higher than necessary, long, straight hair tied back from her face and hanging over her shoulders. Malka Kaplan, her ID showed. Barak was sickened but resigned, since he hadn't found any other solution.

"What's the story?" Funny accent. Assumed, as if she felt she had to pretend to have authority over him, or false expertise. He tried to ignore it and plough on.

"This man, Asaf Levitt, is the suspect in a murder case. He was found with the murder weapon in his hand, dammit. If that's not proof, I don't know what is."

"Did he deny it?"

"No, he didn't say anything. Not one word. Not even when I told him he could ask for legal aid, or I could phone his parents."

"Does he understand Hebrew?"

"Course he does. He's as Israeli as you or… He's as Israeli as I am."

"Is he stupid?"

"No. He's an engineer in a hi-tech company. They say he's very clever. But a loner – you know the type."

"Why did he do it?"

"The man he's… err…suspected of killing was promoted on Thursday. Our Asaf was passed by. Typical story of a loner storing up his hurt for years until one day it snaps."

"I understand. Can I see him now?" She fished a plain, dark jacket out of her backpack and put it on over her uniform shirt, covering any signs of rank.

Thirty minutes later, she returned with a smile on her smug face. Barak wished he had a sponge to wipe it off. Or better still, he'd throw a whole bucket of water at her.

Instead of sitting on the chair opposite Barak, she turned it round, rested one foot on it and leaned over towards him from above, while Barak made a mental note to have the chair cleaned after she left. "Have you heard of social anxiety?"

"No."

"It's basically a fear of people. A sufferer of social anxiety is particularly afraid of what other people think of the sufferer."

"Are you saying our Asaf has social anxiety?"

"He has it in bucketfuls."

Barak's hands were again itching to get hold of a bucket of water. Dirty water.

"His whole life is controlled by it. Everything he does or doesn't do is ruled by this rock that hangs from his neck."

"Why won't he talk?"

"All people frighten him – some more, some less. The ones who frighten him the most are those in authority – teachers, bosses…"

"Chief Inspectors?"

"You've got it."

"How can I get him to talk?"

"You can't. He's marked you out as someone who's high up in the pyramid. He might talk to someone he sees as being on his level – a young, inexperienced police officer, or another prisoner."

"Or someone who pretends to be one."

"That's your business."

"Did he commit the crime?"

"It's not my job to find out such information."

"Look, I planned a holiday. My wife is waiting for me. I want to know if I can wrap this up quickly. Off the record, what do you think?"

She leaned even closer to him, as if about to tell him a secret, but her voice became no quieter. "Off the record, does your wife have a lover who can go with her?"

Chapter 5: Sceptic

Nathalie stopped dead at the sight in the living room.

"Oh, do please close the door," Yarden called from somewhere on the floor. "You're making a draft."

"And you're making me disgusted," said Nathalie, closing the front door and turning the key while wiping her boots on the only corner of the mat free from other shoes. "How can you live with that mess?"

Boxes, folders and piles of loose pages filled the living room floor. Still holding the coat and boots she'd removed, Nathalie ventured around the clutter to come knee to face with Yarden, who was sitting cross-legged on the rug. A laptop perched on the thigh of one leg, her foot tucked beneath the other thigh.

"I have no choice," said Yarden, flicking a lock of curly hair from her eye. "This is my project. I have two-and-a-half days to organise everything and submit it. Two-and-a-half days." She held her hand up above the assortment of articles surrounding her and stuck up two fingers with another half up. "I don't know how I'm going to manage." She looked up at Nathalie, as if she thought salvation would come from her.

"Stop looking so helpless. You've had two months to do this."

"Yeah, but you know how it is."

Nathalie didn't know. She'd always worked diligently and consistently at university. Those frantic all-nighters that were common for some of her fellow students, they weren't for her. But she had an idea. "I'll tell you what. I'll help you with your project if you help me with something."

"You'd better tell me more about the something before I commit. And what are you doing home at this time?"

Nathalie popped her boots and coat into her room and padded back, with slippered feet, to sit on the rug next to Yarden. "Those two things are connected, actually. I'm home because they closed down the office after what happened there."

"What did happen there?"

"Just a murder."

No amount of nonchalant shoulder shrugging could fool Yarden.

"What! Really? Do you mean that?"

"Unfortunately, I do."

"Tell me the whole thing, from the beginning."

"It all started when I got to work, this morning…"

By the time Nathalie had accounted for her morning, so far, Yarden had relieved herself of the laptop and was gazing at her flatmate, open-mouthed. "Wow, Nathalie. I don't know how you can hold yourself together after that."

"Neither do I," Nathalie replied. "Either it hasn't sunk in yet or…"

"Or what?"

"Or I'm so fixated on what I have to do that I can't let myself fall apart."

"What do you have to do?"

"Isn't it obvious? I have to help Asaf and get him out of police custody."

"To help Asaf? But he's the murderer!"

"*Shtuyot bemitz agvaniot*!" Yarden didn't bat an eyelid, but Nathalie felt very clever at being able to use this expression she'd learnt recently, literally 'nonsense in tomato juice' but meaning 'utter nonsense'. "Asaf is no more a murderer than I am. They took the wrong person."

"If he didn't do it, he'll tell the police that and, if they believe him, they'll let him go. Why do you need to get involved?"

Nathalie shook her head. "You don't know Asaf. He won't speak up for himself and they'll think that means he's guilty."

"What makes *you* think he's not?"

"He's such a gentle, quiet soul. He wouldn't murder a fly."

Yarden glanced at her friend with a discerning eye. "You're in love with him, aren't you?"

"I don't know. Maybe."

"And maybe, because you're in love with him, you can't see what he's really like. Maybe he's misleading you. People aren't always what they seem, you know."

"You don't have to tell me that. I learned that lesson at the age of five."

"What happened then?"

Nathalie raised her shoulders. "I'll tell you another time. Right now, I have more pressing things to worry about. I'm positive about this: Asaf is innocent, he's in trouble, he won't stick up for himself, and he needs my help. And that's why I need yours. Please do this for me and then I'll have a look at your project."

"What do you want me to do?"

Nathalie gave a broad smile. "I knew you'd agree." And she popped a kiss on Yarden's cheek. "Basically, we have to find the real murderer so that Asaf can go free."

"How are we going to do that?"

"We'll start off by finding out all we can about the people in the office."

"Okay." Yarden retrieved her laptop from the floor. "I think this is a waste of time, but let's put your mind at rest and then get back to my project. Who's first?"

"We could start with the boss, Gidon Regev."

Yarden typed and turned her screen towards Nathalie. "Which one is he?"

Nathalie looked at the two Facebook search results and pointed to the image of a middle-aged man, his head held high, with a confident, close-lipped smile.

"Okay, let's see. Married, two kids. He goes ballroom dancing. Did you know that?"

"No, why would I? And how is this helping?"

"I suppose we're looking for a connection to Ido, apart from the office one."

"Then maybe we should look up Ido first. Then we'll know if we find someone with a connection."

"Good thinking. What do you know about him?"

"He's very… He was a very sociable kind of guy, friendly with everyone, including those at the top. They all liked him."

"But you didn't?"

"I don't know. I felt there was something sneaky about him. But it was just a feeling."

Ido turned out to be newly married with a baby on the way. He'd changed his Facebook status from 'divorced' only a month ago.

In no time, Yarden transferred to Google and picked one site from a list. "Now this is interesting." She started to read a newspaper article written about eighteen months before, and Nathalie shifted closer to her, to read a little of it over her shoulder. The sea of Hebrew characters made the going tough. She searched for a significant word and found it: *samim* – drugs. Then Yarden explained. Ido, who had been living in Lod, had been suspected of dealing in illegal drugs, but was never charged due to lack of evidence.

Yarden turned back to her friend. "I bet this has something to do with the murder. But drugs are a nasty, risky business. Nathalie, you need to keep out of this. For your own good."

"On the contrary. I need to help Asaf, because by a terrible mistake he's got himself involved in something deadly dangerous."

"Deadly indeed."

Chapter 6: Cell Talk

Asaf curled up on the hard bed, completely covered by the blanket. Next to him, on a wooden chair, stood a tray of food. He hadn't eaten any of it, not even after they told him the sausages were vegetarian.

"Eat," said the big, muscly, tattooed man. "They don't take kindly to hunger strikers, here."

"I'm not…" came a muffled response.

"Oh, for goodness' sake, take your head out of that fucking blanket and talk properly."

The blanket lowered.

"I'm not striking. I just can't…can't face the food. It would make me puke."

"Don't eat, then," said the man. "We don't need to add to the stench in here."

Minutes passed. Asaf's fingers clutched the blanket on his lap, as if itching to lift it back over his face, but a glance at Tattoo Man stopped him.

"How's it going? Did they get the truth out of you?"

Asaf shook his head.

"So you managed to stick to your story?"

Another shake.

"What, then?"

"I didn't…say anything… I couldn't…"

"You didn't talk at all? The whole time?"

Shake.

"What about legal aid? Telling them to phone someone to tell them you're here?"

Asaf shook his head and blinked furiously.

"Oh dear. Oh deary me. You're in for it now. No one's gonna help you. It's you against the whole system. And you're not much use, by the sound of it."

Asaf lowered his head, rubbing his eyes with the blanket.

"Why couldn't you talk?"

"He had three diamond shapes on his shoulder. I don't know what that means exactly, but I know that three leaf signs in the army is a colonel. I've never spoken to anyone so high up."

"They're only ordinary people underneath, you know."

Asaf shook his head. "I couldn't…"

"What happened the second time?"

"It was a woman, younger, no stripes or anything."

"Did you talk to her?"

"Sort of. I sounded ridiculous, but I said something."

"Did she get the story out of you?"

"She didn't ask about that."

"Oh yeah? What did she ask?"

"About my life up to now. About feelings and things."

"Oh my god. I'm sharing a cell with a loony. They're going to lock you up in one of those loony bins…sorry, mental hospital. Just keep away from me, I'm warning you."

Asaf didn't look as if he had any intention of getting close to the man. In fact, he moved back as far as he could and pulled the blanket over his head.

Not long afterwards, they came for the man. "Say goodbye to your friend," someone said. And the big guy come over and tapped on the blanket. "Goodbye, weirdo. Take my advice and own up. You'll be better off."

"Goodbye," said Asaf from inside his cocoon.

Asaf lowered the covering just enough to see the big guy lumbering over to the guard at the gate. Then the guy raised his arms, wide apart, palms up, and shook his head. Pointing to his own head, he twisted his forefinger. A smirk appeared on the guard's face.

Left alone for the first time since leaving his flat – could that really have been this morning? – Asaf was finally able to think with a clear mind. Yet, try as he might, the events of the early morning were still a strange blur, from the moment he opened the little cupboard that contained the alarm, wondering why the light wasn't flashing. The next thing he remembered was a scream. A piercing, screeching scream. He felt as if he'd been in a trance before that and the scream woke him up. The first thing he saw was his hand on the handle of a knife, while the other end of the knife was pushed into a body with the face of Ido. He remembered thinking this couldn't be real. Then he turned to see Sagi's shocked face, and Gidon, who came into the office just behind her. What had happened in those in-between moments, between opening the cupboard to turn off the alarm and standing there over the body, holding the handle of the knife? Why couldn't he remember?

Gidon had taken control, telling Sagi to go and sit down, pulling Asaf's hand from the knife and calling the police. In no time, sirens heralded the police, who rushed in, and Asaf found himself handcuffed to a policeman in the printer room. Yes, he was pretty sure all those strange things had happened, yet he couldn't remember those first few moments in the office.

He frowned and tried winding the memory video further back, to the time he woke up and turned off his alarm. Today was going to be the first day of his new life. Today, he was going to stop hiding and stop everyone from ignoring him. Today, people were going to notice him. Today, everything was going to be different, like the song, like both songs. But it was meant to be different in a good way – not like this. What went wrong? How did he end up in a detention cell? None of today made any sense at all.

Somehow, he'd got himself stuck in a cell with no hope of getting out. Ever. He couldn't talk to the important police chief and he wouldn't be able to talk to the judge. And no one in the world would stick up for him. A lack of alternatives meant he'd learned to do everything for himself and by himself. And now, in this place where he couldn't do anything for himself, he was stuck because he had no one else.

He slumped on the bed. He felt locked inside, not just physically locked in the cell, but also inside himself. The latter was nothing new, of course, but it was the cause of all his current woes. It was why everything had gone wrong today. Oh, how he longed to wipe out today and return to yesterday. He would even return to Thursday. He'd thought that day was bad, but it was nothing compared to today.

Asaf stood up and rubbed his face. He tried a few stretches. No. What could bring those moments back? He wandered around the cell, examining his surroundings. Stark, roughly painted walls, once white, were now covered in stains. Except for high above. There, on the wall opposite, was a small window covered with thick metal bars. He carried the wooden chair over and stood on it on tiptoe. The view was disappointing. All he could see was a high stone wall. But sounds reached him. He heard the general background noise of the city and occasional hooting from cars. A siren, too, from an emergency vehicle, faint but clear.

Beyond the wall, hard as it was for him to grasp, normal life continued. He closed his eyes and saw cars edging forwards, their drivers impatient to reach their destinations. He saw people walking, some quickly, with a sense of urgency, others dawdling, chatting together. Out there, people were free to do as they pleased while he was stuck in here.

Wasn't this what he was used to? Peering out of the window of his single room at the street above. Watching life going on without him. People chatting, smiling, laughing. What did it matter if he was in that prison or this one?

No. There, he had comfort and freedom. He was free to leave at any time, to go to work, to buy food, to go out for a walk or to watch a show. He had the choice to do whatever he wanted – to be alone or to socialise.

What he chose to do was to turn his home into a prison. He prevented his heart from over-beating by cutting himself off and immersing himself in loneliness. That was his choice… His only choice. He shook his head at the metal grille. It wasn't a choice at all.

But this was worse. This was enforced and regimented. Compulsory socialising on their terms. How could he survive it?

He had to find a way of telling them he didn't murder anyone. Maybe he could hold a large banner at the window. What would he write on it? He'd write **HELP** in big letters and underneath it would say **I'M INNOCENT**. Then, if someone happened to look over that wall, they might see it. Could that happen? He very much doubted it. And even if they did see his banner, they wouldn't do anything about it. He didn't blame them. He wouldn't have acted on such a plea either. He'd have thought whoever wrote the note was crazy. He used to think the police knew what they were doing. That if they arrested someone, then he was probably guilty. And that if they found they'd made a mistake, they'd soon release him. He never thought the person in the cell could be someone like him, someone who couldn't stand up for himself.

He had to face up to it. No one would help him. He was going to be stuck inside forever. They'd hold some trial, in which they'd find him guilty, and they'd sentence him for life. His life was over, all twenty-seven years of it. From now, all he'd have would be an existence.

He wondered what proper prison will be like. Full of violent, dangerous prisoners, he imagined. How was he going to manage to get on with them? He couldn't even get on with decent people. It was going to be beyond awful. That much he knew.

How did that psalm go? From where will my help come? My help will come from the Lord, who made heaven and earth. He hadn't prayed for a long time, but in the present circumstances, he was willing to try anything. Anything at all.

A key turned in the lock. "Don't even think of it." The commanding voice made Asaf fall over in his rush to jump down and return the chair to its place. Not that it would make any difference. As if he wasn't in enough trouble, now they thought he was trying to escape. He sat back on the bed and picked up the blanket.

Another prisoner was left in the cell. Asaf saw a slim young man before dragging the blanket over his head. When he peeped, the prisoner was sitting in the corner, rocking and groaning. Asaf tried to ignore him and did a bit of rocking, himself.

After a while, the man started talking. "I don't know how it happened. I was just walking along the street and they nabbed me. Said something about a robbery. I told them they had the wrong man, but they wouldn't listen."

Slowly, Asaf pulled down the blanket just enough to be able to see the man in the corner. He looked to be in his twenties, like Asaf, with a babyish face, his hair neatly cropped. And also like Asaf, he'd been brought in for a crime he didn't commit.

Asaf, knowing the only thing he could do for the other man was to tell him he wasn't alone, ventured two words. "Me, too."

"You too, what?"

"I didn't do what they think I did."

"What was that?"

Asaf put his hand to his forehead. Did he want to tell his tragic tale to this stranger? He seemed nice, yet they'd only just met. But Asaf had already told the big guy, and this one would surely be more sympathetic. Desperate to be understood, he took the plunge. "They think I murdered someone."

"Oh no! How awful! Why do they think it was you?"

Finally. The big guy had clearly thought Asaf was guilty. Barak also seemed to think so and Asaf let him carry on thinking it. The woman didn't talk about the crime, itself. But this other prisoner – he actually believed him. The confidence he showed towards Asaf enabled Asaf to find the words to answer his question. "They found me with the murder weapon in my hand. But I didn't do it."

"Wow. Sorry, I didn't introduce myself. I'm Nadav." He didn't move from his corner.

Asaf nodded.

"What's your name?"

"Asaf." Asaf knew he should have given that information before. He always knew after the event what he should have said or done, but never managed to do these things in time. No – that wasn't true. Most of the time, he didn't know at all. He'd missed learning the social norms that came to everyone else so naturally. Still the man – Nadav – didn't seem put out by Asaf's lack of manners.

"Pleased to meet you, Asaf. Although it could have been under better circumstances."

Asaf nodded. The circumstances were not great. He could not deny that. His future looked decidedly bleak. And yet, this one-to-one conversation with someone who treated him as if he was normal made it difficult to look as if he really agreed about the circumstances. The corners of his lips kept trying to turn up into a smile. He had to push them down and push his lips up in the middle as he nodded. He hoped he didn't look ridiculous.

"So this weapon, what was it?"

"A knife."

"Why was it in your hand?"

Chapter 7: Checking Out the Workers

"Right," said Yarden. "So we know that Gidon has a family and does ballroom dancing and Ido had a shady past and was probably involved in drug dealing. No connection, yet. Who's next?"

"Omer Cohen. Deputy manager. Nice, friendly, laid back."

"Could he be into drugs?"

"Do I look like someone who knows?"

"Yikes!" Yarden exclaimed as the screen flashed up. It's going to be hard to whittle down all these Omer Cohens. Let's leave him for later."

Kfir turned out to be a real goody-goody. Progressive Judaism, synagogue volunteer, charity-giver, the works.

"He doesn't sound like a murderer," said Nathalie.

"That could be what he wants you to think."

"What do you mean?"

"All that religion and charity and so on. That could be a cover. So that you don't suspect him of killing anyone."

Nathalie frowned, then shook her head. "You wouldn't say that if you knew him. With Kfir, what you see is what you get. It's that simple – *he's* that simple."

Sagi, the secretary, turned out to be a budding author. She recently wrote a novel in a month in some crazy sort of online rush. She posted her word count every day, and her friends cheered her on.

"I thought authors did more than just count words. Isn't it more important to concentrate on finding the right words?"

“Someone made a comment like that.” Yarden scrolled down. “Here it is. Sagi replied, explaining that this is a good way to finish the first draft quickly. Afterwards, there’s loads of editing before anyone else is allowed to read it.”

“Okay. That makes a lot of sense. What sort of novels does she write?”

Yarden clicked a few times. “The one she just completed is a murder mystery.”

Nathalie raised her eyebrows. “Wow. You don’t think… I mean, she couldn’t have murdered someone in order to get material for her books, could she? No author would be that stupid, right?”

Yarden left the question hanging before turning back to her laptop. Carmel was only twenty-three, just out of university, steady boyfriend. Reut, married with two young kids.

“Reut is always made up to the hilt. She really tries it on with the men,” said Nathalie. “Even Kfir looks like he’s fighting with himself when she’s around.”

“And Asaf?”

“Not Asaf. Reut can’t get through to him because he’s too locked up in his little cage.”

“Or cell?” Yarden suggested.

Nathalie let out a sigh. “He must be going crazy in there. We’ve got to get him out.”

“Or prove that he should stay in.”

“Yarden, I told you he’s not guilty.” Nathalie sounded fierce.

Yarden leaned to her side of the rug. “Okay, I take it back. You’re not usually so touchy.”

Nathalie winced. “I’m sorry. I didn’t get much sleep last night. And now all this.”

“Let’s have a meal when we’ve done this. Is that everyone?”

“There are two others. One’s away, the other is on sick leave.”

"Or so they say. Presumably they both have keys to the office and could have been there."

"You're right."

Yarden checked out the other two. The one on holiday was walking with his hiking group by the Dead Sea. There were pictures. The one on sick leave definitely appeared to be coughing and sneezing and running a temperature, according to her Facebook status and the friends who had visited her.

"So that leaves us with the elusive Omer Cohen. Laid back, you say. Could be the result of getting high?"

"Wait, I forgot Charlie. He's a freelancer, but I think he has a key because he works funny hours."

"Charlie what?"

"Charlie's not his real name. People call him Charlie because no one can be bothered to say his real name, but I've seen it written, because I have to contact him, sometimes. It's Vyacheslav Preobrazhensky."

"Russian?"

"How did you guess? He's the systems guy. They call him in when they need him to fix a computer problem or get a new computer ready for use – that sort of thing. I only saw him a couple of times."

"What's he like?"

"Not what I expected. Short, middle aged, black fuzzy hair, strong Russian accent, jovial, good sense of humour."

"You like him, then?"

"Yes and no. I didn't like the way he laughed at Asaf. And I told him so. I think he concluded that I don't have a sense of humour."

Yarden typed his name when Nathalie spelled it out.

"Single. He has lots of friends, most of them in or from Russia. He writes to them in Russian."

"Why wouldn't he?"

"No reason, but I don't understand Russian. There might be some connection to drugs in what he writes, but we wouldn't know."

"You could try that **See translation** option."

"I don't think that would help. Druggy words usually have innocent meanings, too. I'd recognise them in Hebrew, maybe in English, but I think any hidden meanings here would be lost in Russky."

"Okay. Where does he live?"

Yarden copied the name and pasted it in the phone book. She gasped when the next screen flashed up.

Just then, Nathalie's phone rang.

Nathalie glanced at the screen. "My mother. Wait a minute, I'll get rid of her. I mean… You know what I mean."

Yarden nodded, a grin lightening her face as she listened to an increasingly frustrated, tone-rising voice, despite understanding nothing between "*Bonjour, Maman*" and "*Au revoir, Maman.*"

"Yes?"

The sigh was almost a groan. "My sister's pregnant."

"Aren't you happy?"

"Of course I am, but I happen to be busy just now, and my mother wouldn't stop talking. About August being a good month to give birth, and they don't know if it's a boy or a girl but Brigitte said she'll take either."

"Huh?"

"It was meant to be a joke and I didn't laugh properly. Can we carry on now?"

"Hey, calm down."

"Where were we?"

"Your Charlie and his address."

"Oh yes. I thought he lived in Jerusalem. Where's Savyon?"

"It's only the most expensive place to live in the whole country. It's in the centre, not far from Tel-Aviv. Anyone who lives in Savyon is rolling in it. Especially if they live in a villa."

"*Mon dieu!* He once mentioned that his home was a villa. I thought he was joking. I mean, he's Russian, and the way he looks, he's the last person I'd expect to be rich."

"He's not just rich. He must have billions."

"Where does all that money come from?"

"He might have inherited it."

"That's one possibility. Or he might be involved in drugs."

"Not as a user."

"No. He could be the big boss. The one who manages all the others and never gets his hands dirty himself. Now that I think of it, he could be the type to do that. I can see him taking charge and giving orders. His work in computers could be a cover."

"What if he *is* the big boss? Does that help us at all in solving the murder? He wouldn't have been anywhere near there."

"But he'd know what happened."

"And if we go there, all the way to Savyon, and ask him, he'll be sure to tell us, won't he?"

Nathalie nodded. "You're right. He'd be too clever to let on that he had any connection."

"So, whether he's into it or not, I think we can leave him out of our search."

"That brings us back to Omer again. And, I just remembered… When Barak the police chief announced that Asaf was being taken into custody and would be arrested, everyone gasped except for Omer. I wondered if that was because he knew something the rest of us didn't."

"You know what I think? If all roads lead to Omer, surely, once we get to that junction, there'll be a signpost that tells us where to go from there. Unless the junction is the end of the journey."

Chapter 8: Cellmates

"I took the bus to work as usual this morning and then walked to the office," said Asaf. Nadav had told him exactly how his arrest had come about. He'd also said plenty about his background – how he'd struggled at school and was fed up with his poorly paid grocery delivery job. It was only right that Asaf should open up to him. Besides, Asaf felt he'd burst if he kept the trauma to himself any longer. He had to grab this opportunity. "I went into the building, up in the lift and walked round to the office. I took out my key and opened the door. I took the key out, put it in my pocket and closed the door. Then I rushed to open the little cupboard to tap in the code that turns off the alarm, but the light wasn't flashing as usual. I didn't know what that meant. Then I must have turned round and… I think that's when I saw it. It was so strange I couldn't believe it was real."

"What did you see?" Nadav asked, his voice quiet, his head to one side.

"Someone was lying on the ground, face up. When I got close, I saw it was Ido, a guy who works in the office. Something was sticking out of his body – a knife. I panicked. There was no one else there. I didn't know what to do, but I was sure I had to do something."

Suddenly, the fog lifted. While relating the story to Nadav, the first person who clearly believed him, Asaf could see himself in the office, looking down at the body with the knife, his heart hammering against its walls, his breaths short and fast. And he knew what happened next.

“I got hold of the knife and tried to pull it out. I know it’s a stupid thing to do, but my brain wasn’t functioning then. That’s when they came.”

“Who?”

“Gidon, the boss. And Sagi, the secretary. She came in first and screamed. I remember hearing it as if it was in the background, or a long way away. There were all these noises going through my head and this body on the floor with the knife, and my hand was on it. I’ve never felt so confused.”

“How awful. So these two people – Gidon and Sagi – arrived straight after you?”

“Yes… no… I don’t know. It’s all so hazy now. I don’t know how long I stood there looking down at the body. I wasn’t thinking straight.”

“No, of course not.”

They fell into silence for a few minutes. Then Nadav spoke again. “There must have been a lot of blood on the floor next to the body.”

“Yes. Well, no, not when I first arrived, but when they found me there holding the knife, it was everywhere – on the floor, on my hand, on my clothes. I couldn’t understand where it all came from.”

“That’s terrible, Asaf. It makes my ordeal sound like nothing.”

“Thank you for listening to me – and believing me. No one else believes me.”

“How d’you know that?”

“The policeman who interviewed me. He shouted at me. I couldn’t stand it. I turned away from him and covered my ears to block out some of the noise. He made me put my hands down.”

"Tell me about the interview. Did you manage to tell him what happened?"

"I didn't manage to tell him anything. Not one word."

"You mean after the formalities – name, ID number, address."

Asaf blushed and looked down. "I didn't answer those either."

"Why not?"

"I saw his uniform when he came into the room. Three diamond shapes on his shoulder. I thought he must be really high up in the force. And his whole demeanour fitted that. Brusque, no-nonsense. I felt I was wasting his time."

"So you didn't answer the simple questions?"

"It's not that I didn't want to. I couldn't. His presence made me unable to speak. I couldn't even think straight. I felt sick and very frightened. He got more and more frustrated with me and there was nothing I could do. He shouted something like, 'Tell me everything that happened to you, today,' and, 'How did the knife get into your hand?' It was awful."

"Oh dear."

"Then he brought out a note I wrote last night and put in my trouser pocket. It says, 'Today will be different.'"

Nadav gasped. "He must have thought it meant you were planning the murder."

"But I wasn't. It was nothing to do with that. It was…oh, never mind. The note belonged to a different life. Now I've been locked away and I'm never going to be able to get out."

"But you're innocent."

"It's not enough to be innocent. I have to be able to tell the police and then a judge. I can't do that." Asaf blinked back the stinging tears.

Chapter 9: Juliette Beauchamp

They sat at the kitchen table, each with half a pita filled with hummus, tomato and onion, and a mug of instant soup. Not Nathalie's favourite meal, especially as the hummus came in a tub and didn't have the special taste of a restaurant-bought variety. But it was available and quick to prepare, and time was rapidly evaporating.

Yarden sat with one leg folded under the other. "Let's go through this again. When did the murder take place?"

"This morning, before anyone arrived at the office. I don't know exactly what time it was. Probably around seven o'clock."

"But there must have been two people in the office – Ido and the murderer. Does Ido usually arrive early?"

"No, Asaf is usually the first one in. Everyone knows he's the one who opens up."

"So that's one question that needs to be answered: why was Ido there early this morning?"

"You're right. I hadn't thought of that."

"What's Ido's wife like?"

"I don't know. I didn't even know he had one… Yes, I did. I remember him saying one day that his wife wasn't well, and he needed to buy food on the way home. Why d'you ask?"

"She might know why he was at work early today. I think you need to ask her."

"Why would she tell me that?"

"She probably wouldn't tell Nathalie Weyl, newest employee at Gidel Electronics. But she might tell…Juliette Beauchamp, private investigator, especially if Juliette is kind and considerate and awfully sorry to disturb her at such a sad time."

A cheeky grin grew on Nathalie's face. "I've always wanted another identity."

"But remember I warned you against all this. Remember I told you it's much too dangerous and you shouldn't get involved."

***

The flat was in a run-down block in Stern Street. Rehov Stern, Yarden had informed her, used to be known for being a street no one wanted to live in, if they had a choice. Yarden had grown up in Jerusalem and knew these things. But she added that the city was in a constant state of change, and Rehov Stern was no longer what it used to be.

Opposite the block, a sign pointed to a park. Nathalie wished she could visit it, but decided she had more urgent things to do.

The long, three-storey block was sandwiched between two taller ones – one under construction, the other being renovated. Clearly, the area was being transformed, but this block was one of the originals, put up in a hurry, and faced with grey stone, before the law that required all buildings to be covered in the lumpy Jerusalem stone.

The block was built on pillars and had four entrances. Nathalie examined all of them, to get a feeling for the place and courage for her mission. Each entrance had an open room to the left and a padlocked room to the right. The latter, she assumed, had to be the bomb shelter, mandatory for every building in the country. There were also stairs leading up and, behind them, an open area. There were no flats on the ground floor, but the entrances, open rooms and spaces behind the stairs contained a variety of objects. Nathalie saw a double pram, a bike, notice boards, rubbish including disposable coffee cups, and a table with a plastic table cloth trying to cover books, pages and old voting slips.

Nathalie couldn't help comparing it to the block containing her own shared and rented flat. Here, the overall feeling was one of neglect. Nathalie's flatmates complained about their maintenance fees, but at least their building was clean.

Time to switch. I'm Juliette, she thought, and I live in a luxury apartment in Mamilla, where the floors are spotless at all times. As she climbed the two floors, stepping around the dirt, she noticed all the front doors were strong, security doors – the type with metal bars inside. Was that a clue that the residences on the other sides of the doors were in a better state?

Sudden darkness caused her to gasp. Why did the lights on staircases never stay on for long enough? Fortunately, she'd just reached the second-floor landing. She groped around on the wall until her fingers found the switch that restored the light.

The sign on the door read Ido and Hila Bitton. It was opened by a short, stocky, middle-aged woman. She kept the chain on and peered round the gap, frowning at the young woman outside. "Yes?"

"I'm so sorry I have to bother you at this terrible time, but I'm afraid that's part of my job." The young woman put on a serious but friendly expression, hoping to break the ice. "I'm Juliette Beauchamp, private investigator." She flashed an ID card at the woman. It was Yarden's student card.

The woman placed her hands on her hips and looked ready for a fight. "She's not ready to talk to you people."

"I understand. But you see…" Juliette glanced sideways and lowered her voice. "We believe the police are missing important evidence in this case. We believe it's important to see justice done and find the real culprit."

One hand descended. "But she's too upset to talk, poor child. She wouldn't even talk to the woman who came round to help – the social worker."

"Are you her mother?"

"I am."

"Would you let me ask *you* some questions? I won't be long. It's important." Juliette pleaded with her eyes.

"I suppose so." The woman removed the chain and let Juliette in, closing the door behind her.

First step passed, thought Juliette. She took a notepad and pencil out of her bag. They stood in the hallway. Juliette winced at the peeling walls. She wished she had a bucket of paint to slap on them. Steady on, Juliette. Don't forget on the stroke of midnight, or some other time, you will turn back into Nathalie, who has to return to a home with peeling walls.

"What is your name?"

"Aviva Atias."

Juliette scribbled. "Thanks for agreeing to this, Aviva."

She nodded.

"How long have Hila and Ido been married?"

"Only two months. He got her pregnant. I told her to get an abortion, but she wouldn't. I told her to leave him. I said I'd help her with the baby. She said she loved him and wanted to marry him."

"Why did you think she should leave him?"

She shrugged. "Mother's intuition. There was something wrong with that man. I just knew it."

"Anything in particular?"

"He was Moroccan, for a start."

"I'd keep quiet about that one if you want people on your side." When Aviva said 'Moroccan', Juliette knew she didn't mean he lived in Morocco or even that he'd once lived in Morocco, but simply that his parents or grandparents had come from there. Aviva was probably of Middle-Eastern heritage, possibly Iraqi.

"He left her alone a lot. Went off to important meetings, or so he said. He had a desk full of papers she wasn't allowed to look at. There were all sorts of things going on in his life that he kept secret. Not a good start to a relationship, that's what I think." Aviva raised her chin as she finished talking. She looked like someone used to having her thoughts noticed.

"Was he hard to get on with?"

"No, not at all. He was always friendly and talkative. He could talk my hat off. If I was younger, he'd have talked my knickers off. That's what he did to my poor Hila."

"May I look at those secret papers?"

"Be my guest, but don't take any away. The police want to see them, too. They said they'd send a locksmith over."

Aviva showed Juliette into a dark, poky bedroom, in which a massive old dark desk against the opposite wall took up a considerable amount of the space. It was impossible to miss it, but Aviva pointed it out, anyway. "Here it is." She reached towards it, palm up, spreading out her fingers, as if introducing someone.

Juliette approached the desk and tried the drawers. Only the small one at the top opened. Juliette, of course, knew how to pick locks, but Nathalie didn't, and this posed a difficult problem as Aviva stood by the door, watching.

The top drawer contained only pens, pencils, a ruler and a pile of envelopes. Juliette felt the envelopes, one by one, until she came to one with something hard in it. She opened the envelope and was delighted to find a small, shiny key, especially when it magically opened the other drawers.

The papers in the bottom drawer confirmed Juliette's suspicions. Ido had been dealing in illegal drugs in his spare time. Juliette got out her camera – her phone – and photographed three telling documents.

The other two drawers showed why Ido needed the extra cash. He'd been married twice before and fathered four children. The sums he had to pay out were considerable.

Juliette took some more photos and then turned to Aviva. "It would really be very helpful if I could talk to Hila. And possibly what I have to tell her now will help her over her grief more quickly."

Aviva nodded and led the way to the living room. A girl looked up at them, tears streaming down her face. She couldn't have been more than eighteen. Her stomach bulged and looked fit to burst. "No," she screamed. "I can't talk to anyone. I just can't."

Juliette sat next to Hila on the worn sofa and spoke softly and gently. "Don't talk, just listen."

The girl sniffed and nodded.

"I've just been through your husband's papers, the ones he kept locked in the desk."

Hila's mouth opened to gasp. Then it closed.

"Do you know that Ido was married twice before and has four children?"

Hila shook her head. "No, are you sure?"

Aviva, who had brought up a dining chair, said, "I knew something was up with that so-an'-so."

Juliette continued. "Do you know that Ido was dealing in illegal drugs?"

Now mother and daughter both stared at her. Juliette gave them time to take in her news. "May I ask you something now, Hila?"

Hila gave a hardly perceptible nod.

"What time did Ido leave for work this morning?"

Between sobs, Hila replied. "Quarter past six. He said he tried to leave without waking me, but I woke up and he told me he had to go for an important meeting. Then he kissed me and left. That was the last I saw of him." Fresh tears streamed down Hila's cheeks and she laid a hand on her bulge.

"Quarter past six and it's two bus rides from here, so he'd have arrived at about a quarter past seven."

"No," said Aviva. "He had a car. A brand-new Volkswagen Tiguan provided by the company because he had to travel so much."

"I see. Thank you very much for your help, both of you." As Juliette stood up, Aviva replaced her on the sofa, hugged her daughter and tried to comfort her.

"I'm so sorry to have bothered you," Juliette said. "I'll let myself out."

Nathalie left the building slowly, walking down the two flights of stairs and out into the cold, fresh air. It wasn't so nice of her to disturb the poor girl after all that had happened to her, especially as she was about to give birth. Nathalie hoped that what she had told her would help Hila to get over her grief more quickly. With any luck, she would come to realise that she had been wrong about Ido and she should have listened to her mother. She was lucky her mother was there for her, although she probably didn't think so in the past.

Thinking over what she'd just learned, Nathalie reflected on Aviva's statement about the car. A brand-new Volkswagen Tiguan, she'd said, provided by the company because he had to travel so much. But Ido didn't have to travel at all for work, and Nathalie was pretty sure he didn't drive a company car.

As Nathalie stepped onto the pavement, a deafening explosion pierced the air.

Chapter 10: Going Home

It took him well over an hour to walk home. He'd decided it was the best way. The car was no longer available, a taxi too expensive and too dangerous. On buses, other passengers could take too much notice of him. No, better to wander the streets. After all, he looked like a tramp and that's what tramps did.

People stared at him as he trudged along the streets. He saw them even though he kept his head down as much as possible, only raising it occasionally to make sure he was going the right way, like a racing swimmer raising his head out of the water to breathe in. He did mostly find the right way, as he knew the direction he needed, but sometimes he found himself at a dead end, or the road he was on took a sharp turn in the wrong direction.

Still, he noticed. Even with his head down, eyes fixed on the pavements, he felt them. They stared and they kept their distance, as if they were afraid of catching something from him, as if trampdom was a disease. Or were they afraid he'd harm them with an evil spell, or cast an awful stench over them?

He ploughed on, doing his best to ignore not only the stares but also his thoughts about what would happen next. He forced himself to concentrate on getting home. That was enough for now. Later, he would make plans for the future.

It was only when he arrived home that he saw the state of his coat. And by that time, exhaustion claimed him.

Chapter 11: Barak Isn't Happy

Nathalie panicked. The bang seemed to come from inside the building. She ran as fast as she could to the main road and then down the hill, towards the centre of town. Good thing her boots were almost flat. She kept turning back, unsure if she was checking for followers or looking for a taxi. She almost ran into a man coming the other way, but saw him just in time. When a taxi stopped for her, she pulled open the back door and flopped onto the seat.

"You okay?" the driver asked, concerned.

"Yes. I've been running, that's all." She pulled the door closed and fumbled with the seatbelt. Still breathing heavily, she gave the driver her address.

Home came into blurred view with the relief of familiarity. Nathalie paid, then ran up the stairs, collapsing on a chair, panting, cheeks wet.

Yarden looked up from the rug and gasped. "Nathalie, what happened? Did someone attack you?"

Nathalie shook her head.

Yarden extricated herself from the laptop and surrounding mess and approached her. "What then?"

The only sound from Nathalie was of short, sharp breaths.

"Can I get you something? Tea?"

"Don't get too used to this service," warned Yarden, bending down to place Nathalie's slippers by her feet.

Nathalie sipped the hot tea. "What a shame. I was starting to enjoy it."

"That's better. Now you're back to your old self, you owe me an explanation."

"I was just leaving the building when there was this awful bang behind me. I thought…I don't know what I thought. It spelled danger to me. I thought I had to get away, as quickly as possible, and I started running."

"Surely you didn't run all the way home."

"I'm not that crazy. I got a taxi."

"What do you think now?"

"I think someone's trying to harm me. Someone doesn't want me to carry on investigating."

"Can I say, 'I told you so'?"

"You can, but what should I do now?"

"Keep out of this, Nathalie. Murder and drug dealing – this is a very dangerous business. Keep out of it, for your sake."

"But what about Asaf?"

"If Asaf is innocent—"

"Asaf *is* innocent. There's no 'if' about it."

Yarden ignored the noisy interruption, except to smile at the way Nathalie waved her arms when she became agitated. "In the end, the police will work out the truth. They have to."

"Poor Asaf. He must be suffering so much."

"There's nothing you can do about it, Nathalie. Nothing at all."

A knock on the door made them jump. It must have been more of a thump. Yarden opened it and was surprised to see two police officers, one male and one female, who pushed past her and entered the room. The man looked at the woman and inclined his head towards Nathalie.

The woman spoke to her. "Madam, were you in the vicinity of…" Except that she used the word *Gveret* for Madam and made it sound much more disdainful than was possible in

French. Then she gave the correct address in Stern Street and the correct time that Nathalie had been there: two-forty in the afternoon.

"Yes."

"Please come with us to the police station to answer some questions."

"I didn't do anything."

"Then you have nothing to worry about."

Yarden said, "Excuse me, are you arresting my friend?"

"Not at this stage. We are simply requesting her presence to help us with our enquiries. She doesn't have to agree, but that could weigh against her in a court of law if it comes to that."

"Can I come with her?"

"Yarden, it's all right," said Nathalie. "If there's been some misunderstanding, I'm sure I can clear it up, and you've got work to do."

"Well, if you're sure."

"I am."

"But do call me if you need my help."

Nathalie gave a half smile to reassure her friend. Inside, she didn't feel any of that confidence. But she put on her coat and boots and left with the officers.

They didn't talk to Nathalie in the car. On arrival at the police station, they took her in, pointed to a long wooden bench in a corridor and told her to wait there. Then they left Nathalie to try to make sense of her situation. Perhaps Asaf had said something that she could help with. That would be all right. But they'd mentioned the place in Stern Street. What if, for some reason, they suspected her of being involved in the murder? That wouldn't be all right. It would be terrible.

She glanced at her two neighbours on the bench. The man on her left had gashes on his face and blood was dripping from his forehead. She edged to the right, closer to a girl in skinny jeans and a sleeveless top cut so low that it hardly covered anything. The girl kept still and gazed with apathy from an over-painted face. Nathalie wondered why she wasn't shivering. She herself felt cold in her coat and boots.

Eventually, Nathalie followed someone into a room just large enough to hold a rickety table and two wooden chairs. Its roughly painted stone walls looked no better than those of the corridor she'd just left. She gasped when she recognised the man behind the desk.

"You again," said Barak, the Chief Inspector. "Strange how you keep popping up."

"It's only the second time," said Nathalie.

"Sounds quite a lot to me. Not everyone is lucky enough to get to talk to me twice in one day. Have a seat."

Nathalie sat and immediately felt caught in the headlights of Barak's glaring eyes.

"You were seen running away from the scene of an explosion. The building just happened to be the one where the victim of this morning's murder lived."

Nathalie kept quiet. There was no need to affirm Barak's statement. Clearly, he knew it was true.

"You know, there are some murderers who can't keep away from their victims. They have to find out whether anyone suspects them of the crime. If they think someone suspects them, they try to murder that person, too. They're very silly to do that, of course, because they put those investigating the crime onto them, like a dog sniffing a scent. Do you get me, Nathalie?"

"Yes, but if you think that applies to me, you're barking up the wrong tree."

The smirk on Barak's lips was fleeting. "What were you doing at that building, Nathalie?"

"I was trying to help Asaf. I know he's innocent and I was trying to find out what really happened this morning, so that Asaf could be released."

"That's very nice of you to be so loyal, but it's not your job to investigate this murder, and I'm sure those of us who have been given the authority to do so can manage on our own, thank you very much."

Nathalie looked down at her legs and tried to ignore the staring headlights.

"Why did you run away?"

"There was an explosion. I was scared. I thought someone was trying to get me…to kill me. So I ran."

"Are you sure you didn't cause the explosion?"

"Yes. I'm sure."

"You realise that causing an explosion is a serious crime, especially if it's intended to be an attempt on someone's life."

"Yes, but…."

"And if it turns out you've lied to me, that will be another point against you."

"I haven't lied to you."

Barak looked down at some notes. "Tell me about your flatmates."

"I told you about them when we spoke in the office."

"Tell me again."

"There's Yarden, who's studying criminology. And Tehila, who's studying acting."

"What else do they do? Do they have boyfriends?"

"Tehila has a boyfriend."

"Do you know him?"

"I've met him." Nathalie cringed as Barak's face reached closer to hers, making her breaths shorter and faster.

"Would it surprise you to hear that Tehila's boyfriend is hooked on hard drugs?"

Nathalie opened her mouth and closed it.

"Well?"

"I didn't know, but now that you mention it, I can see it would explain some strange behaviour."

"Like…"

"Sometimes he acts sort of crazy. His mood swings from high to low in an instant."

"Where does he get the dope from?"

"How would I know? I didn't even know about it."

"I suggest you do know. I suggest you are his contact with the drug dealers."

"No. You're wrong."

Barak continued to glare at Nathalie until a phone rang. He picked it up and listened. Then he said, "Thank you," and replaced it, slowly shaking his head.

"You're lucky," he said to her. "The explosion was completely unconnected. Caused by a faulty gas cylinder. You're free to go."

Nathalie's relief was tempered by concern. "What about Ido's wife…I mean widow, and her mother? Are they all right?"

"Yes, they're all right. No one was injured by the explosion. But the shock caused her to go into labour. It was the right time, anyway."

Barak stood up and Nathalie followed. "I trust you'll take my advice now and keep away from private investigating."

There didn't seem any need to reply, so Nathalie didn't.

Chapter 12: What the Neighbour Saw

Mazal lowered herself onto her straight-backed chair by the window that overlooked the garden below. The garden belonged to a neighbour, Eran, who lived on the ground floor. She shook her head. She used to like him and his wife. She didn't know them well, but they were always pleasant when they met on the stairs. Sadly, Eran had let himself go since his wife died. He'd let his hair grow long and wild, and now seemed to ignore everyone.

The garden, too, had become overgrown lately, but she still liked to gaze at it. It was better than watching at the street on the other side. The garden was only small, but it had some fine trees, growing lemons, olives and pomegranates. Mazal had told them once how to prepare olives, and they'd been nice enough to give her a jar of them.

In the old days, Mazal was always busy, cleaning houses to earn more money for the family, then coming home and cleaning their own place, and preparing meals, of course. Yes, she used to love cooking, serving out dishes that the family gobbled up – kubeh, sabich, stuffed vegetables, all with different fillings and seasonings. Those were the days.

Now, the children had grown up and had families of their own. They came to visit of course, bringing their own not-quite-so-delicious food, and Mazal felt guilty because she couldn't make the meals she used to make. Even preparing food for her and Shmuel was a strain. She sighed. It was true what they said: old age wasn't for the faint-hearted.

The light was fading. It got dark so early on these winter days, and the sky had been overcast all day. While Mazal watched, she just managed to make out a person moving around in the garden. Must be Eran, she thought, but why would he go there in the evening? Surely if he wanted to tend to the garden, he'd do it during the day, in the light. Yet, he was carrying tools and making for a particular spot, past the lemon tree.

It was getting harder to see and she leaned forward. The man seemed to be digging. Why would he do that in the dark?

"Everything all right, dear?" Shmuel asked, coming in from the kitchen where he'd been washing up.

"Yes. Could you turn the light off, please?"

"Why do you want it off?"

"There's something strange going on down there and it's hard to see."

Shmuel flicked the switch and came to stand beside his wife. "I can't see anything."

"No, it's too dark now."

Just then, a light came on and pointed directly at the place where Mazal was watching.

"Must be Eran, planting something."

"Why would he do that at night?"

They watched whoever it was digging for some time. Then he picked up something from the ground.

"What's that?" Mazal asked.

"Looks like material, or a garment of some kind. Look, he's folding it. Now he's tossed it in the hole he dug!"

"And now shovelling the earth he dug up and putting it back. How odd."

They continued to watch as the man patted the earth down with the spade and then stamped on it. Apparently satisfied with the job, he returned to the building, carrying his tools.

"What do you think that was about?" Shmuel switched on the light again.

"I don't know. It was hard to see what the thing was that he buried. It must have been something he really wanted to hide. Do you think we should tell the police?"

"I don't know. It's probably nothing. We don't want to be thought of as nosy neighbours."

"And we didn't see the person's face. It could have been anyone."

"Yes. Best to keep it to ourselves."

Chapter 13: Curious

"We've got to sort out the other mess first. An innocent man is still locked up, and I can only imagine how he's feeling. I'll tell you what, when we've found the murderer, I'll help you with your project."

"But it's due in the day after tomorrow."

"Then we'd better find the murderer quickly."

"Nathalie, you are the limit. All right, so Ido dealt in drugs, and he went to the office early, probably to meet a client."

"Right."

"And the client was probably Omer."

"Why do you think that?"

"Because he works in the office and he's the only one who sounds likely."

"Just because I said he's laid back? I don't think so. He has his wits about him. He knows what's going on all the time."

"I think you should check him out. I managed to find out his phone number, by the way."

"How?"

"I searched for him among Gidon's Facebook friends, and then used a file I shouldn't really have."

Nathalie raised her eyebrows, but let the matter go. "How should I check on Omer?"

Yarden looked down, her pen against her lips. "Give him a call. Put on an accent so he doesn't recognise you. Tell him you've got a delivery for him and where does he want to meet to collect it. If he sounds confused, he's probably not our guy."

Nathalie shook her head. "I already have an accent and I can't hide it. He'd recognise me straight away. Couldn't you…" She put on the most pleading expression she could.

Yarden managed to hold off for a full two seconds. "Oh, all right."

Nathalie listened as Yarden recited her line. "I've got a delivery for you. Where do you want to meet to collect it?" Yarden's expression remained serious and she added very little else to the conversation. Only after closing the call did she allow herself to gloat. "Told you."

Shocked, Nathalie raised her eyebrows.

"This is what he whispered. 'Entrance to Independence Park from Agron Street – the closest one to the supermarket, one hour from now. I'll wear a dark green woollen hat. Follow me into the park. At a distance. I'll stop at a bench. Don't sit too close. What will you wear?'"

"Is that when you said, 'Red gloves'?"

"Yes."

"But I don't have any."

"I do."

Nathalie screamed. "I can't believe he took the bait. You were right all along."

"I told you. People aren't always what they seem."

Nathalie flopped onto a chair and looked up at her friend. "What do I do?"

"If you're me, you tell the police at this stage. If you're you, you probably go head first into this and meet him."

"He'll recognise me."

"Does that matter? Your work at Gidel could be your cover."

"What do I say to him?"

"You've come to give him something, so… I know." Yarden vanished into the kitchen and returned, tying up a black plastic bag. “Take this bag of rubbish. Don’t give it to him. Leave it on the seat when you get up. They always do that in films.”

“But how does that help me?”

“You have to ask him why he murdered Ido.” She picked up a newspaper that was lying amongst the detritus on the floor. “Here, take this and hold it in front of you as if you’re reading it. Then you can talk to him without anyone knowing.”

Nathalie glanced at the newspaper, dated a week before. Why it was still hanging around was a mystery to her. She left the paper and bag by the front door and went to put on her boots and coat. Yarden retrieved the red gloves from somewhere in her room. How she found anything in that room was another mystery to Nathalie.

As she opened the front door, Nathalie said, “Wish me luck.”

“Good luck, you fool.”

Nathalie took the bus towards town and checked her watch when she arrived at the place. Five minutes to go. It was dark and cold. Street lights brightened the street, but the park was shrouded in darkness. Nathalie shivered and stamped her feet a few times to keep warm. She turned as if to admire the green grass and trees, although, in reality, both were hard to make out. The medium-sized park was bounded by three main streets – Agron, Hillel and King George – and a few minor streets. It was a great place to get away from the bustle of the centre of town. Usually, she loved to take a few minutes to sit on the grass in the sunshine. But not on a day like this.

Nathalie liked the way those three street names, like most of the streets around here, were steeped in history. Her interest in this history had led her to discover the origins and commit them to memory. It helped to connect her to her chosen city. King George Street was named after the British King George V in the 1920s, during the British mandate period. Hillel was a Jewish religious leader from long ago, known as the author of the well-known saying: 'If I am not for myself, who will be for me? And being only for myself, what am 'I'? And if not now, then when?' And Gershon Agron founded the English-language newspaper and had been mayor of Jerusalem in the 1950s.

But now, Nathalie had other things on her mind. She had to agree with Yarden that Omer was the one. She'd never thought of him as a murderer, but she'd definitely noticed something strange about him, something he kept hidden. It was hard to pin it down. He was always very friendly and talkative, but she felt there were things he didn't talk about. Yes, he had to be covering something up.

So, that was it. He was involved in this drugs business and, for some reason, things got violent, that morning. Or else, he always intended to kill Ido. She didn't know which, but she was determined to find out.

Her heart beating fast, she kept looking out of the corner of her eye. A few people walked past. No one else stopped. Then she spotted him standing, the green hat perched above most of the passers-by. He didn't look in her direction, yet when she turned to face him, he moved away with an air of determination and proceeded into the park. Nathalie waited a few seconds, then followed him.

Omer sat, with one long leg folded over the other, at one end of a bench and opened up a newspaper, holding it in front of him. Nathalie did the same at the other end, putting the black plastic bag beside her.

"So, it's you." Omer's voice was soft but clear. "I wondered about you."

Nathalie pushed the plastic bag towards him and asked her question. "Why did you kill Ido?"

Nathalie watched Omer out of the corner of her eye, and caught a look of utter shock. "I didn't…" Abruptly, Omer folded his newspaper, put it under his arm, stood up and strode away from the spot, towards the Hillel Street exit. The black plastic bag remained on the seat.

Nathalie frowned, confused at what to make of this. She scrunched up her newspaper, picked up the black plastic bag of rubbish and tossed both into a nearby bin on her way back home.

***

"What does this all mean? It doesn't make any sense." Nathalie was back on the rug beside Yarden, but now her fists were closed, her knuckles white. She'd been on the edge of a breakthrough when suddenly it all screwed up and fell apart.

"The whole business is very odd, I agree," said Yarden. "He seemed to take the bait, knew what you meant about the delivery, but when you asked him why he killed Ido he walked away."

"And he started to deny having done it." Nathalie frowned. "Time for another think, I guess." She lowered her head, tucking it between her knees, and circled all with her arms. Then she looked up and spoke with deliberation. "I think our Omer is up to something else on the side – not drugs. I think it all hinges on the word delivery. It was a bad word to use – too vague. A delivery can be anything. Maybe he's waiting for something specific. Who knows what? He could be some sort of spy. He thought I was involved in that, but suddenly he realised I was something to do with Ido, so he had to get away from me before I blew his cover."

"Nathalie, your imagination is running away with you. You've been reading too many spy stories."

"Well, maybe. But Omer isn't the murderer. That look of shock on his face was too real."

Yarden sighed, loath to admit defeat. "I suppose you're right. But if he isn't, then who is?"

"I think we need to look at the others again. We must have missed something."

Chapter 14: Trained to Fight

"Okay, Reut the Tart, married, two young kids. What else do you know about her?"

"She always comes dolled up, too much paint on her face, cleavage visible but decent. I wonder how she manages it with the kids and everything. She's short. Claims the high heels are a necessity. I can't see her thrusting a knife into anything, let alone a human being.

"And Carmel?"

"The complete opposite. Tall, big. Always comes in trousers with flat shoes."

"Anything else?"

"She seems a bit lost, fed up with her life, now. I remember her telling me she did her army service in a unit called…'Carcal', is that right?"

"The Caracal Battalion. Wow."

"What is it?" As an immigrant to the country, Nathalie had not been drafted. In a way, she felt she'd missed out on this experience shared by most of those she met.

"It's an infantry battalion that's mostly female."

"And they learn to fight?"

"Of course."

Recognition came to the two friends at the same time. Each saw it on the other's face. Yarden expressed it.

"Large, trained to fight, bored with her life, maybe depressed. She did it."

"What's her motive?"

Yarden shrugged. “What’s her surname again?”
“Bronstein.”
Yarden did some more typing. “She lives with her parents and seems to be fairly well off.”
“How do you know?”
“She spent the summer touring in America. Look, here are the photos.”
“Oh yes, I remember she mentioned it.” Nathalie looked through the screens of miniatures. “I see she did it in style. Luxury hotels and enormous cars.”
“Right. And look at this post. It says, ‘Fabulous all-night party. The Americans really know how to live it up.’”
“Hmm. What happens in all-night parties?”
“I don’t know. I’ve never been to one, but…”
“Wouldn’t there be a lot of sleeping around?”
“I guess there could be.”
“And wouldn’t they take something to get into the mood first? Something not exactly legal?”
“Possibly.”
“And if one attended a few of these parties in quick succession, couldn’t one get hooked on this substance that wasn’t quite legal?”
“Certainly.”
“If that happened to Carmel, then when she came home she’d probably look for a source for the substance.”
“*If* that happened.”
“And that source could well turn out to be Ido.”
“Nathalie, you’re jumping to conclusions again. The likelihood of all that happening is about point zero zero one out of a hundred.”
“I think it’s more than that. I think it’s worth giving Carmel a visit. If we start off talking about the murder, we could move on

to other things. America, for instance. That's a country I'd love to visit. I wonder what it's like…"

"Big," said Yarden.

***

Shira perched on a kitchen chair in their two-storey dwelling, known as a cottage, in the neighbourhood of Gilo. This was, by no means, the first time she'd been in this situation, her immediate future hanging in the balance. Fortunately, she no longer had to worry about kids nagging her for answers she didn't have.

Through the open door, she could see the two small suitcases, one black and one blue, waiting by the front door. What were they waiting for? To do the job they were designed for, holding the clothes their happy owners would need on arrival at their distant destination? Or would the cases end up being returned back upstairs, stripped of their contents and dumped back in the storeroom? Judging by previous experience, Shira thought the latter option much more likely. She sighed.

But just in case, she went through her mental list. Swimming gear, snorkels, suntan lotion, hats, underwear, evening wear. Yes, she was sure it was all there. She glanced at the clock. Not much time left. Barak would phone her, she was sure. He wouldn't leave her in the lurch. Then her phone rang and she answered it.

When she finished talking, she went to the hall and heaved one of the suitcases up the stairs. "One day," he'd said. "I promise you. It will happen sooner than you think."

Shira dropped the suitcase onto the floor and went back down for the other one.

***

Nathalie had often wandered the streets of Yemin Moshe, or sat on the grass at the top of the neighbourhood, or examined Montefiore's windmill, the replica of his carriage and the surrounding paths. She loved this peaceful, traffic-free neighbourhood. Built on a hill, it afforded magnificent views of Jerusalem's Old City and the dwindling surrounding countryside. Today, she squeezed past a group of Israeli tourists concentrating on the words of their guide. Moses Montefiore, the British philanthropist after whom the neighbourhood was named, featured prominently in the talk. When it was over, she heard some of the group singing a song that included the name Montefiore and made a mental note to find the song and listen to it.

Despite her occasional visits, Nathalie had never been inside one of its dwellings, but she'd heard visitors discussing the exorbitant cost of buying property here and was looking forward to this opportunity.

From the outside, the house looked pretty large. Inside, it was a maze of nooks and crannies, a mixture of old and new. Arched windows and doors broke up cream painted walls, which were decorated with photographs of all sorts, neatly spaced. Carmel hung Nathalie's coat in a well-polished, fitted wardrobe in the impressive entrance hall. Then she led the way, on a floor of large shining tiles, along one wall of a spotlessly clean kitchen that looked positively out of this world. A central, silver-topped island contained sinks and electric rings. One long wall was completely covered in light wooden storage space and an enormous, silver-coloured fridge. The opposite wall and the one at the end were made of stone bricks. These must have been the outer walls of the original house, one of several built under Montefiore's providence at the end of the nineteenth century to encourage residents to move out of the poor and crowded walled city.

"We'll have privacy in here," Carmel said as she led Nathalie from the top of the stairs into a large bedroom with a floor of polished wooden tiles. Nathalie swivelled around, taking in the private bathroom, the walk-in closet and the door to the balcony. "Have a look at the view," Carmel added.

Nathalie stepped out to look down over red roofs to the panorama before her. Exquisite, but today was too cold for lingering. She shivered and returned to the warmth of the room. "You're so lucky," she said.

At one end of the room, an L-shaped sofa covered in burnt orange material welcomed them. Folding one leg over the other, Nathalie relaxed against one of the sofa's arms. Carmel, on the other end, twisted her large frame to face Nathalie and rested an arm on the side and another on the back of the sofa, stretching out her long legs. She looked very much at home here. "I'm so glad you came. I've been feeling weird about this whole thing. I mean, it's not every day you're involved in a murder, is it?"

'Involved in a murder.' An unfortunate turn of phrase?

"No. I wasn't sure you'd want to talk about it, after they told us not to. But it's hard, isn't it? I mean, you need to talk. We all do."

"The whole thing is such a shock. I mean, okay so he was weird. But I didn't think he was going to kill someone."

"Right, I still can't believe it either." Nathalie wanted to keep this conversation amicable, to make Carmel believe she was being supportive and friendly. "What do you think is going to happen now?"

"How do you mean?"

"Do you think the company is going to carry on as if this episode is just a blip that we can all forget, or is this the end of Gidel Electronics?"

"That would be a shame, but there are plenty of other companies to work for."

"Yes, I've been thinking it might be an opportunity for me."

"In what way?"

"I haven't been working for long and I haven't been able to take a holiday yet, but I have a friend in California who would love me to visit. If Gidel closes down, I could go there before looking for another job."

"Good thinking. I've been so anxious about the murder, I haven't thought past it."

"I've never been to America before. Have you?" *Please take the bait.*

"Yes, in fact I toured America last summer. I had a great time."

"Oh yes, now I remember you saying. Where did you go?"

"All over. New York, Washington, San Francisco, Florida, lots of places. I have friends and family there, so I got to see plenty of people."

"Were they young people?"

"Some of them, yeah."

"Did you get to sample the nightlife there as well? All night parties and stuff?"

"We went out a bit, but nothing like that."

"Oh really?"

"Yeah. But I made up some all-night parties for my friends on Facebook. You know how you always have to exaggerate on Facebook, otherwise people think you're a nerd or something."

"Yeah, of course." Nathalie hoped she sounded as if she'd done the same sort of thing on Facebook, although really she'd never felt the need to tweak her persona. Time to change the subject. "Anyway, I'm sure you have everything you need here. You've got such a beautiful house."

"My parents do, yeah. It's convenient and comfortable and hard to get away from."

"Do you want to get away?"

"I'd like to, yes. If I could find a job in Tel-Aviv, I could be more independent for a while before settling down. I've lived such a sheltered life up to now, except for the army, of course.

Maybe if my job here ends now because of this mess, it'll be an opportunity for me to try that. On the other hand, I don't know how I'd broach this to my parents, and my boyfriend wouldn't be pleased, either. Between you and me, he's quite a bore and I'd be happy to ditch him, but that would be hard, too, because my parents like him."

Nathalie had let Carmel waffle on, but now was time to guide her to a more useful topic. "Are you worried about starting out on your own?

"I am, but if you don't take risks in life you never get anywhere."

"I'm worried, too, living here away from my family. I think I'm most worried about getting dragged into drugs."

Nathalie watched Carmel's face. Her expression looked shocked and serious with no hint of a cover-up.

"I don't think many people get *dragged* into drugs. If you're strong and say *no* to the pushers, you can keep away from them. No way would I want to start with them. I value my life too much."

Returning to the apartment, Nathalie contemplated the puzzle. Suspects were dropping off the list like olives had, a couple of months ago, from all the olive trees. Rather than feeling closer to the truth, she felt she was getting further away from it. Only one thing was she sure of, now as much as ever, and that was Asaf's innocence.

"We've drawn a blank again," she said, walking through the door. "She…" Nathalie stopped in amazement. There, relaxing next to Yarden on the sofa, facing the mess of Yarden's project, was the least likely person she could have imagined.

Chapter 15: On a Role

"Omer!" said Nathalie as soon as she felt able to. "I didn't expect to see you here."

"I thought I'd better give you an explanation for my strange behaviour today," said Omer. "Both of you, in fact, as I understand you're working together on Asaf's behalf."

"Yes, that's right." Nathalie removed her coat, slung it over a chair to save time and drew another chair over to sit opposite the other two. Omer leant back on the sofa and stretched his long legs out in front of him, reminding Nathalie of his pose in the conference room when Barak announced the murder.

"You see," Omer continued, "like you, I believe Asaf is innocent. And, like you, I caught on to the drug connection. In fact, I was following a lead that I don't think I should tell you about just now. So, when you phoned, I thought it was in that connection. I thought you might be connected with the murder, but then I realised you thought I was the murderer, and my first reaction was to walk away from the scene before the misunderstanding caused some sort of violence. Now, after investigating further, I know that you're not the murderer or anyone connected with the murderer, so I'm no longer afraid to discuss this with you."

"I see," said Nathalie. "Have you also worked out who the murderer is?"

"No. I'm afraid I haven't managed that yet. I've only got as far as eliminating people I thought might be connected." Omer rose. "I'm sorry I can't stay any longer. I just wanted to clear that up and apologise for my part in causing the misunderstanding."

"Thank you for coming and explaining. Won't you stay and have a cup of coffee? We could continue the investigation together."

"No, thank you. I work better alone."

When Omer had left, Yarden said, "Well, that clears that up then."

"Does it?"

Yarden frowned. "He gave an explanation, didn't he?"

"Yes. Only trouble is, I don't believe it."

"Why not?"

"The whole explanation sounded not quite right, but the last sentence can't be true. He works better alone? I've never seen that in the office. He's always discussing things with other people, making plans together, and so on. He's usually such an open person, it doesn't make sense. I think… Oh, never mind."

"No, tell me."

"You'll say I'm crazy, but…say I'm right and he is a spy. He would need to give us an explanation for walking away as he did so that we don't go telling the police that he might be a suspect. That's why he came up with this story for us, but I think my spy version sounds much more likely than the one he just told us."

"Nathalie, you're crazy, but it doesn't matter. Whatever the truth is about Omer, he's not our man. How did it go with Carmel?"

Nathalie shook her head. "She's not our woman. She was completely honest about everything she said to me. I'm sure of that."

"Oh dear, she was our last hope. We've run out of possible culprits. Are you sure it wasn't Asaf all the time?"

Nathalie glared at her friend.

"No. All right. We'd better think again."

Silence reigned for a minute or two. Yarden broke it. "We're missing something, probably because we're stuck in a box we need to break out of."

Another minute passed until Nathalie shouted. "Yes, that's it."

"What's it?"

"All this time, we've been assuming something that might not be true."

"What?"

"That the murderer must work in the office."

"Because no one else has a key to the office."

"Why did the murderer need a key?"

"To surprise Ido when he came in."

"What if Ido let him in?"

"Why would he do that?"

Nathalie's hands waved in excitement. "Because he doesn't know the man's a murderer."

"Or woman."

"He lets this person in because this is where they arranged to meet. He told his wife he had an early morning meeting, and for a change he wasn't lying." Nathalie was on a roll.

"Why in the office?"

"Why not? Ido knows he'll have privacy until Asaf arrives at seven thirty."

"He can't be expecting a fight, then."

"No, it's just a meeting. But it turns nasty."

"Where did the knife come from?"

"I don't know. It would help if we knew what the knife looked like. How can we find that out?"

"Asaf would know."

Nathalie sighed. "But Asaf is locked up."

"He could have visitors, couldn't he?"

"Maybe, but someone would be listening in to the conversation. And then they'd know we were investigating."

"Two other people saw the knife – Gidon and Sagi."

Nathalie frowned. "How do you know that?"

"I forgot to show you. While you were out, I checked for any news. There's a long article about the murder. Long, repetitive and not very informative. But it does say that the manager and the secretary discovered Asaf with his hand on the knife."

"*Mon dieu*, they mention Asaf by name?"

"No, but you know how it goes. At the beginning they refer to a nameless man and soon afterwards they say 'We can now reveal the name…'"

"When that happens, people will read the article and think Asaf is guilty. How's he going to live with that?"

"How does anyone live with it?"

"Yarden, Asaf isn't anyone. He's sad and alone and his self-confidence is so low it's on the floor. He's not going to stand up for himself. He'll let them continue to accuse him, even though he's innocent."

"Yeah. Let's get back to the task in hand. Gidon or Sagi. Which one are you going to ask about the knife?"

Nathalie groaned. "Gidon is the big boss and Sagi would never agree to tell me."

"Why not?"

"We were told not to discuss the murder between us. I don't see her breaking that rule."

"And Gidon?"

"He's the boss. Why would he talk to me?"

Yarden bit her lower lip, then let it go. "I think Gidon needs to be visited by a certain private detective."

"Not me. He knows me."

"Nor me. I'm terrible at acting."

"We need an actor who doesn't know Gidon."

The front door opened and in came someone who wore a cheerful grin and long braids.

"Tehila," the other two chimed together, wide smiles brightening up their faces.

"Well! To what do I owe this wonderful welcome? Have you two been missing me? Aw, that's so touching."

"We're just happy to see you, Tehila," said Yarden.

"Oh yeah? And what's in this for you?"

"Nothing," said Nathalie, jumping up. "As you say, we missed you. Let me get you a nice hot cocoa. And by the way, out of interest, what are your plans for this evening?"

"I thought I'd have an early night. Curl up with a book." Tehila gave an exaggerated yawn. "There's this murder mystery I'm reading…"

"Talking of which, we were thinking of a little acting job for you. It doesn't pay anything, but it would be great experience."

"What do you mean?

"Right," said Yarden as Tehila left to complete her mission. "You're going to help me with this project."

"What?" Nathalie stood up, tipping her chair over. "When Asaf is still locked up and we're no nearer to finding the real murderer? I don't have time for that, now."

"Then you'd better find time. I've wasted more than enough helping you."

With a sigh, Nathalie bent down to pick up the chair and carried it back to its place by the table.

"And bring some coffee while you're up."

The look that passed from Nathalie to Yarden could have been mistaken for aggression, but these friends knew its true meaning: *I owe you this.*

"So what's this project about?" Nathalie asked as she set the mugs down amongst all the mess on the floor.

"It's about various aspects of forensic science. If we can categorise these pages into sections, I'll be able to write a table of contents, and then I might be able to see what's missing."

"Wouldn't it have been easier to plan the whole project from the beginning to know what you had to write?"

"Probably, but I didn't do that and now I only have one day left."

Nathalie shook her head in despair. As always, Yarden needed a maid to tidy up after her. Nathalie was tired of that role.

Half an hour in, when Nathalie had received a description from Yarden of most of the pages, something caught her eye. "Hey, look at this."

"What?"

"This page. About the profile of the criminal."

"What about it?"

"Well, don't you see? It could help in finding Ido's murderer if we know the sort of person we're looking for."

"Nathalie, you're supposed to be helping me organise the project."

"I am. But I have to understand all the parts before I can put them together, and this part looks interesting."

"Nathalie..." Yarden rolled her eyes.

"Here. Look, you listed the types of people who become drug addicts."

"I know I did. So what?"

Nathalie understood her friend. After all, she'd lived with her for three months. Yarden wasn't stupid and knew where this was leading. She was simply doing her best to put off the inevitable.

"If you'd asked me, I'd have said a drug addict was basically a weak person. He'd be...or she...someone who was introduced to drugs socially, couldn't say *no* and couldn't stop once they started. But I see there are lots of reasons. Trauma, abuse, mental illness, chronic pain… Look at this one: loss of a loved one. It could happen to anyone. If someone they love dies and they don't get the right help, they can look for something to ease the pain."

"Yes. Post-traumatic stress disorder. It comes up all the time in this course."

"Do you ever stop to think about the meaning of all this stuff you're learning? These are real people suffering from stress and not getting the help they should get."

"You're right. But I don't get to see these people. They're just theoretical for me."

"Well, maybe this is when they become real. Or when one particular one becomes real."

***

Hagit Malada, partner of Juliette Beauchamp in their unnamed company of private investigators, flashed another multi-purpose card at Gidon. This one showed the right picture if not the right profession or name. Hagit didn't give him time to notice these discrepancies as she talked her way into his luxurious apartment situated in Talbiyeh – a stone's throw from Yemin Moshe, though not quite as exclusive. "We suspect – that is, our client suspects – that the police have been too hasty in their assessment of this crime, and that's why we've been called in."

"Who is your client?"

The manager spoke with confidence, sounding as if he was used to getting his questions answered. Hagit wasn't intimidated, although Tehila had to put all her acting skills into operation to carry that off.

"I'm afraid I'm not at liberty to divulge that information."

"I see. What do you want from me?"

"Just to ask a few questions, if I may."

Gidon sighed. "I suppose."

He led the way into a tastefully filled living room. Hagit sank into a flower-patterned cushion and took out her notepad.

"I understand you were the first in the office after Asaf."

"Sagi and I arrived together. Sagi used her card to open the door and walked in first, I was just behind."

"What did you see?" Hagit was writing furiously.

"Asaf bending down to a body on the floor. The handle of a knife was in his hand and the other end was inside the body. If that's not proof, I don't know what is."

"Proof of what?"

"Proof that Asaf murdered Ido. Besides, he was that type."

"What type?"

"The type to turn to murder. You read about them all the time. Loners who can't stand their miserable lives any more, so they decide to end them in a spectacular way."

"Tell me about Asaf."

"As I said – a loner. Brilliant engineer but impossible to talk to. I could never get a word out of him. I wanted to dismiss him because he didn't fit in our team, but Omer disagreed. He got on with him a bit better than I did, and found him useful."

"Did you recognise the knife?"

"At first, I couldn't see it properly with half of it inside the body and the handle covered by Asaf's hand. But afterwards the police showed it to me, and I said it looked like the cake knife from the office kitchen. Then we searched and found it was missing, so that must have been it."

"Can you describe it?"

"It's long and sharp with a pointed tip and a black handle."

"Why did you need a pointed tip for cutting cakes?"

"I don't know. I don't handle that side of things. Sagi is responsible for buying equipment of that sort."

Hagit made sure to get a receipt from the taxi driver who dropped her beside a tall building in Ramat Sharett. This was definitely a valid expense that she would claim from the unnamed company. She got through the security door when someone came out, then took the lift to the sixth floor. It was a guess because, in typical Israeli style, there was no correlation between the flat numbers and the floors, and no indication in the lift. Fortunately, she only needed to walk up one more flight.

Her ring was answered by an old man in a button-down cardigan who welcomed her in. She didn't even have to flash a card at him.

"Sagi is very upset about what happened."

"I'm not surprised," said Hagit. "She must have had a terrible shock this morning. And I'm really sorry I have to disturb her, but this is most important, I assure you."

"Wait a minute. I'll see what she says." The man vanished into a room and soon returned. "She'll see you," he said. "Please be gentle with her."

"Don't worry," said Hagit. "I have experience of these situations."

As Hagit entered the living room, Sagi, who was sitting on an armchair, started to rise.

"No, don't get up." Hagit pulled the other armchair closer to Sagi and sat down. Sagi was slim with short, curly brown hair. Her long face was streaked with tears. "I won't keep you long, but this is very important."

"That's all right."

"The knife that was used in the office for cutting cakes."

"Yes?"

"Did you buy it?'

"No. Actually, Ido bought it. He said he needed to buy some kitchen equipment for his house, and he might as well get the knife, too. He didn't even ask for any money. Wasn't that nice of him?"

"Yes. But why did he buy one that's sharp and has a pointed tip?"

"I asked him about that. He said if you're getting a knife, you might as well get one that's good for other purposes. Just in case."

"In case of what? Surely you never need to carve meat in the office."

"No, of course not. I don't know what he was thinking of, really."

"What do you think happened this morning? Do you think Asaf could be the murderer?"

Sagi shrugged her shoulders. "When we found him there with the knife in his hand, it seemed obvious that he'd done it. But afterwards, thinking about it, I wasn't so sure. I know he's quiet and a loner and all that, but underneath it he seems like a nice guy. I really can't see him as a murderer."

"Thank you, Sagi. You've been very helpful."

Chapter 16: Three Heads

It was almost ten by the time Tehila returned to the flat with her new information and three receipts for taxi rides. Nathalie winced but paid up. Her friend had performed well.

"That's great," said Nathalie. "Now we know that Ido bought the knife."

"Right. And I'm going to do what I planned to do two hours ago and curl up in bed."

"No, not yet. I still need your help."

"In the morning." Tehila disappeared into her bedroom.

"And I've got a project to get on with," said Yarden.

"Oh no, you don't. I spent time helping you. Now I need your help to work this out."

"Work what out?"

"Why did Ido buy the knife that killed him – a knife that was especially sharp with a pointed tip?"

"I don't suppose he meant it to kill him."

"So he meant to use it to kill someone else?"

"Or at least to threaten someone."

"Who?"

"Good question. It doesn't seem like anyone who worked in the office. I think your Ido must have arranged to meet someone else, and he took out the knife just in case the other person turned violent."

"But somehow the other person got the knife off him and stabbed him instead."

"Brilliant."

"But who is our mystery person?"

Like bowling pins after a good roll, four shoulders fell together. Glumness pervaded the looks that passed between the two women.

"Stumped again."

"Isn't there any clue in those pages you photographed?" Yarden asked.

"Let's have another look," said Nathalie.

Yarden connected the phone to the computer and they examined each photo that flashed up.

"These are all about Ido's links to the drug providers," said Yarden. "What about his clients?"

"There were lots of names with addresses and phone numbers. I couldn't photograph all those while the mother stood there waiting for me."

"One of those names is probably the murderer. We have to find a way of picking him out, or at least whittling the list down."

"Are we making a mistake by assuming the murderer is male?"

"The vast majority of violent crime is perpetrated by men. I learned that in my forensic science course. When a woman wants to kill someone, she nearly always chooses a non-violent method, like poison."

"Okay. So we're looking for a man of any age, colour or appearance."

"Right. How are we going to get a description?"

"The guard!"

Yarden nodded. "Under our noses…"

"There is always a guard sitting at the entrance. He'd have seen if someone came in or out."

"Who was on duty this morning?"

"I nodded to the guard as I went in. It's the one I've talked to before. His name is Volodia."

With a sudden movement, Nathalie sprang up and pulled her phone from the cord, hurriedly pressing buttons. Seconds later, she looked down at her friend, glum-faced. "Recorded message. I won't be able to talk to anyone at the front desk before tomorrow at six thirty."

Yarden glanced at the time on her computer. "Good. We need to be alert tomorrow. Let's go to sleep now and get up early."

"*Oh là là!*"

Nathalie sat up, took some deep breaths and lay her head back on the pillow. This was getting to be a habit she didn't care for. The dream, though similar to the previous one, bore some marked differences. Asaf's face appeared only for an instant before it changed to another, with a beard and long straggly grey hair and staring eyes. Throughout the dream, she heard the sound of a heartbeat. Boo-boom, boo-boom, boo-boom. It made the dream even more scary and yet she had a strange feeling of calm. As if she was looking back from the future and she supposed – or hoped – that meant the future was rosy. "*Mais ce n'est qu'un rêve,*" she warned herself. It's only a dream.

Sleep wouldn't return, so she buried her feet in her furry slippers, donned her dressing gown and removed herself to the kitchen for a change of scene and a hot mug of tea. She was pouring boiling water into the mug when she heard footsteps.

"Yarden, what are you doing here at half past four in the morning?"

"I could ask you the same thing."

Nathalie replaced the kettle and sat down, warming her hands on the mug. "I had a dream – a nightmare. It involved Asaf. It was scary."

Yarden flicked the switch on the kettle and fished out a teabag from the box in the cupboard. "I was also thinking about Asaf, and feeling guilty. That's why I couldn't sleep."

"You? But you don't know him."

"I know him from everything you've said. What you're doing for him is urgent and important, and I was mean enough to make you spend time on my silly little project."

"Yarden, I couldn't have managed without you. You deserved my help – I mean it. That's what friends are for."

Yarden poured her drink and sat at the little table opposite Nathalie. "What happened to you when you were five?" she asked. "You said that's when you discovered that people aren't always what they seem."

"My best friend at school – we were together all the time and we told each other everything. She told me her father was abusing her sexually. She didn't put it like that, of course, but that's what she meant. I thought she was making it up. I knew her father. He was always so nice to me. Anyway, she said it was a secret and I wasn't to tell anyone, and I thought I was being good by keeping her secret. But I should have told. Years later, when we weren't friends any more, I heard he was convicted of abusing several girls. I told you I learned the lesson that people aren't what they seem at age five. But that's not really true. I learned it when the truth came out."

"You don't blame yourself for that, do you?"

"Well, yes. She must have suffered all those years. And the other girls…"

"You were only five."

They sipped in silence until more slippered feet pattered in. "Ooh, a midnight feast…or as near as makes no difference. Can I join in?"

"Be our guest," said Nathalie. "What brings you here?"

Tehila began to prepare a drink. "Worry, I guess."

"About Asaf?"

"No, about Tom."

"What's up?"

Tehila brought her mug to the table and drew up the third chair to sit between the other two. “He disappeared for three days. I phoned and messaged, but he didn’t answer. I even phoned his office, but they didn’t know where he was either. Last night, I finally got hold of him, but he wouldn’t say what happened to him or where he was. I asked about his work and he said everything’s fine and his boss didn’t mind. It doesn’t sound right. I think he’s lying to me.”

Nathalie took another sip and held the mug to her lips, relishing the warmth on her face and hands. Should she tell? Yes, this time she should. He hadn’t even told her not to.

“I heard something about Tom.”

“You did? What did you hear?”

“After I interviewed Ido’s wife, there was an explosion and the police thought I’d caused it. Amongst other things, they told me Tom was hooked on hard drugs and suggested I was his provider. Then it was cleared up and they let me go.”

Tehila stared at her mug. “I suspected something like that. Thank you for telling me.”

“What are you going to do?”

Tehila sipped slowly. “I haven’t known him for long. It sounds callous but he’s not my problem.”

“I think you’re right.”

“Tehila,” said Yarden, “you were worrying about Tom for three days. Why didn’t you tell us? You looked like your usual happy smiling self all that time.”

“I’ve learned that it’s better to keep smiling and not inflict my troubles on others. People like me that way. They don’t want to hear the sad things.”

“But we’re your friends. That’s what friends are for.”

“Yes and no. I could have told you about Tom. But there are other things you couldn’t understand.”

“Like what?”

"Like what it's like to be black in Israel."

That silenced the other two. Until Nathalie said, "Really? Is it so different? I mean, I don't treat you differently, do I?"

"No," said Tehila. "You're great, both of you. It's the ones who don't know me who see me as different and call me names like Chocolata and Janet Jackson."

"I noticed that," said Yarden. "But you always laugh it off, as if it doesn't affect you."

"Do you expect me to start a conversation on racism with every stranger I pass in the street? And I do understand. Having black people in the country is still quite new. Even though I was born here, some Israelis hardly ever come across people like me. They don't mean to humiliate us, but that's how it feels sometimes."

Silence reigned as the other two internalised all this.

Tehila continued. "I think it's harder for men. Occasionally, the police suspect them because of their skin colour and that can lead to violence. I know it's nothing like as bad as America here, but still."

"We should talk to each other more," said Yarden. "We say we're friends, yet we act like strangers. Let's be here for each other."

"Starting with Nathalie," said Tehila. "Let's put our heads together and solve this murder."

Chapter 17: A Whiff of Freedom

Asaf twisted and turned on the hard mattress, his head throbbing. No way would he be able to sleep. It wasn't the mattress – he could get used to that. It was all the tangled thoughts fighting for attention. He needed to get a hold on them, but there were too many, pulling in different directions.

Just this morning, things had seemed so different. He'd walked to the office full of determination to take real control over his life. Suddenly, in a series of incidents that felt anything but real, all his control had slipped away, removed by complete strangers. It was scary, the power these people had to take everything from you in a single moment.

So, what *had* gone wrong?

The events of the morning were still hazy. It had helped to talk to Nadav, until they'd come to take him away. Wasn't it strange how often prisoners came and went in this place? Nadav had wished Asaf well and told him he needed to talk to the police. Yeah, right.

Asaf remembered entering the building and saying good morning to the guard. Yes, it was an actual 'good morning' rather than a nod, because this was the day everything was going to be different. He groaned. It wasn't supposed to be *that* sort of different.

Asaf remembered going up in the lift. Then he got to the door to his office. Yes, he remembered that, too. He unlocked it as usual, and immediately on entering swivelled to open the little cupboard on the wall to turn off the alarm. That was always uppermost in his mind on entering the office, because if he didn't turn it off promptly, the security company would phone, and it would be up to him to deal with them. But this time the light wasn't flashing, meaning that someone else had switched the alarm off. Yet the door had been locked when he arrived. Maybe someone had forgotten to set the alarm last night? That was his final logical thought, because he turned around and that was when he saw it, in the centre of the lobby.

A body with a knife stuck in it. It looked so surreal. At first, Asaf had thought it must be a dummy. He went nearer for a better view.

How long did he stand there staring at it? Asaf had no idea. It could have been a second or five minutes or longer. Did anything happen during that time? Eyes closed, he forced himself to concentrate.

Now Asaf could see himself frozen on the spot, unable to move in any way, but… Suddenly, a sound reached him – a sound that he heard then but was unable to react to it, paralysed as he was by the sight in front of him. From behind him, someone ran to the door, threw it open, and escaped. Asaf was sure of that now. And the steps weren't even. They were more like a heartbeat. Boo-boom, boo-boom, boo-boom. Who would run like that? Only someone with a limp.

No one in the office walked with a limp.

Whoever it was must have been the one who killed Ido. He – or she – escaped and Asaf was blamed. Which meant that the other person was going to get away with murder. Literally. And there was nothing Asaf could do. He couldn't talk about it. If he wasn't completely tongue-tied, he'd be too scared to be able to explain what really happened to anyone. Unless…of course. That's what he had to do in the morning.

Asaf felt calmer after his decision. He might even have fallen asleep for a short while. But soon, he was wide awake again, putting his grey matter into use long before keys turned in the lock and the gate opened.

"Breakfast," said the guard. "Compliments of the chef. He'll be upset if you carry on rejecting his gourmet meals."

"Could I have a pen and paper, please."

The guard opened his mouth in mock surprise. "You can talk!"

Shortly after, the man returned with a pen and a small pad of paper.

Asaf sat on the edge of the bed, resting the pad on his knees, and tried his best to write neatly, despite his shaking hand and the excitement that caused him to try to write faster than he was able to. He forced himself to slow down, feeling as if his performance now would determine his destiny.

Asaf signed the statement and added the date. He read it through again, then folded it. When the guard returned for the breakfast tray, Asaf asked him to give the page to Chief Inspector Elad. Then he lay back on the bed and fell asleep.

About an hour later, they took him for another interview with the Chief Inspector. Just like the previous day, Asaf's voice deserted him.

Barak Elad sat behind the table, Asaf's statement lying between them. "Pity you didn't tell me this yesterday."

Asaf's heart was thumping again. He should have talked to him. By keeping quiet, he'd made it more difficult for the police to do their job, and that was the last thing he wanted to do. But, even if he could have talked yesterday, his mind had been too confused to be able to provide a full account of the episode. He needed all that time to work out the complete truth.

"Tell me this: have you heard of social anxiety?" the Chief Inspector asked.

Asaf shook his head.

"We're releasing you now. I suggest you go home and look it up. I assume you have a computer at home."

Asaf nodded.

"Look it up and deal with it. For one thing, you might find you're not as 'weird' as you think."

Oh yes, he'd called himself 'weird' in the statement, to explain his behaviour.

"For another, next time something even worse could happen to you. Besides, life's too short to spend it alone. It's other people who make life worth living."

Silence.

The Chief Inspector sighed. "We'll give you your clothes back, but you can't wear them because they have blood on them. I don't suppose you have anyone who can bring you something to wear."

Asaf shook his head.

"No. I'll get someone to buy you some items. You'll have to pay for them, though."

Asaf remained sitting in the small room with the rickety table and two wooden chairs. Both his previous interviews had been held in this room, the failed, embarrassing one with Barak and the other with the woman called Malka, the one who made that first prisoner call him a loony. Oh yeah, he saw the connection now. He couldn't think before.

When the door opened and a young man in uniform entered, carrying a flimsy plastic bag, Asaf couldn't help staring.

"Hello," said the man, closing the door and dropping the bag down onto the floor. He sounded a bit sheepish.

Asaf continued to stare.

"Yeah, they put me in the cell as a plant, because you wouldn't talk," said Nadav, or whatever his name was. "Good thing you talked to *me* or you'd still be in that cell." Probably sensing Asaf's continued unease, he added, "It wasn't all lies. I really am called Nadav."

Still, Asaf lowered his eyes and felt his cheeks warming up. What had he said to this policeman he'd thought was a fellow prisoner? Then his eyes rose, alighting on the policeman's shoulder. Only one V shape. Probably quite low down in the ranks.

"Cheer up, mate. They're letting you go."

"I know," said Asaf. "It's just…well, it's all my fault. If I could have explained properly, I'd have saved everyone a lot of time."

"Hey, don't worry about it, mate. Some people are good at talking, others are brilliant electronics engineers."

"It's possible to be both."

"Yeah, but no one has it all. Let me tell you something." Nadav perched on the table, despite its ricketiness, and looked down at Asaf. "I have dyslexia. Do you know what that means?"

"Sort of."

"Nowadays, I live with it. But when I was at school, I couldn't understand why I couldn't spell, and all the kids laughed at me and called me stupid. The teachers, too. They said I was lazy. It took years before I was diagnosed. I really thought I was stupid. Then someone told me to be proud of all the things I did well instead of worrying about what I couldn't do. It fairly boosted my self-confidence. Now when people treat me like an idiot, I tell them about dyslexia and they usually understand. It's good to have a name for your problem. It means you're not alone."

"Thanks," said Asaf. "Thanks for understanding."

"Cheers, mate," said Nadav, handing the bag to Asaf. "When you've changed, report to the desk outside." Then he left.

Sensing the sweet fragrance of freedom, Asaf dressed quickly in the joggers, shirt and a cheap anorak. At the desk, he paid for the new clothes and exchanged the prison clothes for a black plastic bag containing his old clothes. They also gave him the contents of his pockets: keys, wallet and even the note he'd written – the one that expressed such certainty that things were going to change for the better. Why couldn't they have kept the note, he wondered, or better still, burnt it?

Release. What an amazing feeling. To be free to walk, on his own, out of the police station. Free to go in any direction, do whatever he liked. No one pushed him or shoved him or shouted commands at him. He took deep breaths and released them into the cold, welcoming air.

The normality of everything outside was what felt so strange. People walking, talking, going about their business. No one stared at him and his black plastic bag. A young man was giving out free newspapers. Asaf took one and stuffed it into the bag, which he clutched by its top to keep the contents dry. Rain drizzled down and the air felt fresh. Asaf could have taken a bus but preferred to walk, for the exercise to body and mind, to let his newly-returned freedom wash over him. He passed the Jerusalem Municipality, and Yemin Moshe with its windmill. At the entrance to the Liberty Bell Park, he decided to walk through the park rather than along the pavement. The path was almost deserted on this dull, wet day, but the bell welcomed him with its message of liberty, and his stride, as he continued along the path with overhanging, bare branches, was jaunty. Emerging by the petrol station he marched on, beside the renovated old station – that mix of culture and eating places – and through the neighbourhood of Emek Refaim, still marvelling at the normality.

His ordeal was over. Hopefully, he'd soon be able to pretend it never happened, or at least banish it to history, to join the long list of embarrassing incidents that had plagued his life.

By the time Asaf reached his block of flats, the rain had become heavier and he was pleased to get out of it. At the entrance, he passed Zahava Tzipori going out with her shopping trolley. He didn't know many of the residents by name; he hardly recognised any of their faces. But Zahava was different. First of all, she headed the house committee and so they met over payments and other issues involving the block. But more than that, she always had a smile on her lips and an ability to ignore his tendency to say the wrong thing or to say nothing at all. Her eyes always twinkled with a zest for life.

Today, however, no smile graced her lips. Instead, she stared at him with twinkle-free eyes and walked past without saying a word. How strange.

He reached his door, still pondering, and took a moment or two to retrieve the bunch of keys from his trouser pocket below the anorak. Then he chose the right one and pushed it into the keyhole. At the same time, someone went past, screamed and vanished into the flat next door. Had he missed something while cooped up in a police cell? What could have happened in this block?

At least his little flat was as he'd left it – the dishes, now dry, on the draining board, the whole place tidy as always. But when he opened the cupboards, he saw that things had moved a bit. The police must have searched his flat – normal, he supposed, in the circumstances. Did the neighbours know about that? Did they see them arrive in a police car and open his door? Was that why they were behaving so strangely? He'd have to find a way of explaining to them that it had all been a mistake.

Stepping through the entrance hall, Asaf switched on the air conditioner and made sure it was set for maximum heat. 'Entrance hall' sounded grand. Actually, it doubled as a kitchen. With the sink on one side, next to the little bathroom, and fridge and oven on the other, its floor led from the door to the single room.

Asaf examined the fridge. His stock of food was rather scarce. He'd have to go out later to buy some, but the last of the bread and cheese would suffice for now. As he began to eat, he realised how hungry he was and remembered how much time had passed since his last meal – breakfast yesterday, over twenty-four hours ago.

Feeling much better, he got up to make himself a mug of coffee and took the newspaper out of the bag to read as he drank. He put the mug on the bedside cabinet and opened the paper out beside him on the sofa. As soon as he noticed the main headline, a frown darkened his face.

'*Hi-tech worker found dead in office.*'

Two paragraphs down, his name sprang out at him, as if lit up with neon lights, and his picture was there, too.

No wonder the neighbours behaved as they did when they saw him. They must know all about this. And, as he hadn't had much contact with any of them, they judged him without knowing. This was awful. Asaf felt like he was stuck in the middle of a horror movie, with no way out. He rubbed his face. His hands shook as he picked up the mug and coffee dripped on the cabinet. What was he going to do? He certainly couldn't go out of his flat and face the hostility he knew would be out there. And the fear.

This could carry on all his life, couldn't it? People might always think of him as the murderer who got away. How could he go on like this?

Chapter 18: Guard Duty

Nathalie tried the number several times before finally getting someone. "This is Nathalie from Gidel. Who's that?"

"Hi Nathalie, this is Volodia."

"Volodia!" What luck. "You were on duty yesterday morning, right?"

"Yes. Why do you ask?"

"Could I come and ask you something?"

"Yes, of course."

They'd chatted before, drawn by their common new immigrant status. She knew he studied and worked in his spare time. He also cared for his father, who had dementia. Because of their previous chats, she had something to compare his last answer to.

It was happy and welcoming, perhaps too much so. It sounded forced. Was he hiding something?

Volodia was ensconced in a chair behind the entrance desk when Nathalie arrived. As usual, he was reading a book, but he spotted Nathalie and looked up.

"Do you know all the people who work in the building?"

"Yes," said Volodia. "If there's anyone we don't recognise, we ask who they are. If they're visitors, we ask them to sign the visitors' book and leave some sort of ID, and we call for someone to come down and escort them. Sometimes there are workers who are new. I look them up and check our information against their IDs."

"Yesterday morning, what time did you arrive?"

"Six thirty. I don't understand why you're asking all these questions. The police have already been through all this."

"I think they missed something. Was there anyone you didn't know yesterday morning?"

"No. I told the police that. No one from Gidel came in between poor Ido and that creep, Asaf."

Nathalie tried not to react to Volodia's description of Asaf, or even think about it. Instead, she reflected on the phrase: *No one from Gidel came in.* Did he mean that people who worked for other companies in the building entered between Ido and Asaf, or was he hiding the fact that a stranger entered and went to Gidel's offices? If the latter, what was his motive?

"When did Ido arrive?" she asked.

"Six thirty – just after me."

"Did he seem anxious at all?"

"No, he was his usual chatty self."

"What did he chat about, then?"

"Oh, nothing really. Just…you know…small talk."

"What time did Asaf arrive?"

"About seven thirty, as usual. He startled me when he said good morning, 'specially as he never normally says anything."

"You said no one from Gidel came in between Ido and Asaf."

"Right."

"But someone else came in – a visitor – who went to Gidel. Right?"

It was a guess, but when Volodia frowned, tight-lipped, Nathalie knew she was onto something.

"Who was the visitor, Volodia?"

Volodia winced as tears formed in his eyes. "It's been so hard for me here – the studying and working and looking after my dad. No one knows how difficult it's been except…well, Ido.

He sympathised and said he understood, and he'd try to help me. He was a great guy."

"Yes...?"

"Ido said someone was coming for an early meeting. He asked me to let him in and not write down his details. I wasn't sure, but he said it would be all right and no one else would see. He'd been so nice to me, I couldn't let him down."

"Did he pay you to keep quiet?" When Volodia didn't reply, Nathalie repeated her question.

"It wasn't exactly payment."

"Then what was it?"

"He said it was the help he'd promised me. It wasn't bribery."

"So you agreed and someone came and you let him in without getting his ID."

Volodia nodded, his eyes lowered.

"Why didn't you tell this to the police?"

"I didn't mean to lie, but I was so scared I'd lose my job or they'd arrest me and how would my father manage without me? Besides, they'd already caught the murderer."

Nathalie felt sorry for Volodia. She knew that being an immigrant wasn't easy for anyone and particularly not for him. But she felt even sorrier for Asaf, who'd done nothing wrong. "What time did the person come in?"

"About a quarter to seven."

"Can you describe him?"

"I was surprised. He didn't look like someone who would come here for a meeting. He looked old, with long, straggly grey hair and beard, and he walked with a limp. I know there's nothing wrong with having a limp, but the whole picture together struck me as...strange."

"What time did he leave?"

"I was getting more and more worried. Ido had said no one would see, but it was getting to the time when lots of people would come in. Then Asaf arrived at about seven thirty and said good morning, and I wondered if I should tell him someone was there, but… I was afraid."

"What time did the stranger leave?"

"About twenty-five to eight. He kept his head down and hurried as much as he could with the limp."

"You understand that he murdered Ido, don't you?"

"But Asaf murdered him. Everyone knows that."

"Then everyone is going to have to change their minds."

Volodia stared at Nathalie, the colour draining from his face. "You're not going to tell the police what I told you, are you?"

"I don't think it matters whether I tell them or not. They'll find out in the end."

"What do you think they'll do to me?"

Nathalie held up her little finger. "You accepted a bribe to not fulfil your job properly and you withheld information from the police." The next finger had joined its neighbour. "That doesn't sound too bad to me, but I'm not a legal expert. I hope you'll be okay. I'll put in a good word for you if it helps, but you have to start telling the truth. I think you should call them now and let them know what really happened, before they discover it themselves."

Nathalie was leaving the building when her phone rang. She glanced at the screen. What did Gidon want from her? Did he know she'd sent Tehila to interview him? The conversation that followed didn't answer that question, but it rendered it trivial.

"Barak, the police chief inspector, told me you've been doing some investigating of your own into this crime."

"I have." There was no point in denying it.

"Nathalie, you have to give this up. I'm saying it for your own good. Asaf is so obviously guilty. You're wasting your time and stepping into dangerous territory. Stop getting involved and leave the job to the police. They know what they're doing."

"But they don't know what they're doing. They're keeping Asaf in detention and he's innocent. I know him. There's no way he could commit a crime like this."

"Of course there is. It's all so obvious. You can see how he thought, how he planned, and how he carried it out. He must have been depressed and angry over Ido's promotion, and all he could think about was getting his revenge. He had all weekend to decide to act and then plan the action. I don't know how he persuaded Ido to meet him early in the morning. I think there's a lot more I don't know about. I understand drugs were involved. But you see how it happened, don't you?"

"No, I don't. It doesn't matter what you say to me. You can carry on telling me all those bad things. I simply don't believe it – not about Asaf. He's a gentle, kind person, and he would never willingly harm anyone, no matter how they behaved to him. I'm as sure of that as I am that I couldn't harm anyone."

Gidon sighed. "Let me tell you about loners."

Since when were you an expert on loners? thought Nathalie.

"Loners are always on their own. They don't have anyone to chat to, to bounce ideas off, to talk to when something good happens, or when something bad happens. They only have themselves."

"Yes…"

"If they get some crazy idea in their head, there's no one to say, 'Forget it. That's ridiculous. Be real.' So, instead of forgetting it, it grows in their head and becomes all-important."

"But why—"

"They will always get ideas like that because they're miserable. They always have a grievance, and they concoct stupid ways to get revenge."

"I don't think…"

"You don't believe it? You only need to look at the newspapers. They're full of loners who go out on random shootings, or just kill the people they think are against them."

"But…"

"Nathalie, you'd better start believing because it's true. Think of the loner as someone with a screw loose. When the screw finally drops, that's when he goes and performs his act of revenge. Remember the Austrian co-pilot who deliberately crashed a plane full of passengers? Or the numerous Americans who have fired at random in schools? Loners, all of them. And that's why Asaf committed full-blooded murder, and why you need to stop investigating this crime, for your own good."

"I'm sorry, Gidon, but I disagree."

"You sound convinced, but you're wrong. I don't know what else to say to persuade you. You're putting yourself into so much danger. Remember, drugs are somehow involved in this. The world of drugs is fraught with danger – you know that, don't you? Please keep away from it, for your own sake. If you don't care about yourself, then do it for your parents. They'd be frantic with worry if they knew what you were up to. Don't you care about them? Nathalie, answer me."

***

Gidon sighed again as he closed his phone and returned it to his pocket. What were her last words? Oh yes. "Thank you for your concern, Gidon. I appreciate that you're worried about me and I will do all I can to protect myself. However, I am an adult who is capable of taking care of herself, and I will decide what I can and can't do."

Gidon didn't often fail in what he set out to achieve, but he had to admit that he'd failed, this time. He took out his phone and called a different contact.

"Sorry, it didn't work out," he said when the call was answered. "I tried my best."

Chapter 19: The Impartial Reporter

Asaf opened the newspaper beside him on the sofa and twisted to read it. The front page had been bad enough, with his face staring out at him. At first, he'd wondered who had given his photo to the newspaper. Then a hazy memory provided the explanation. He was still in the office, sitting in the printer room, chained to the man next to him as if he might suddenly escape. Someone had come in, told him to look up, and snapped a couple of photos. No wonder he looked so frightened in the one now plastered over the front page of a national newspaper. How was he going to survive this? If he went out now, people would recognise him, unless he could disguise himself somehow. But how?

Along with his name were a few details:

'Twenty-seven-year-old electronics engineer, Asaf Levitt, who works in the office where the crime took place, lives in Talpiot, Jerusalem.'

Asaf gulped. No one could mistake him now. Turning to page three, Asaf found the whole story, as radiated to the world by the media. The reporter who wrote the article purportedly didn't take sides and had made sure to preface all details with 'According to the police', and to call Asaf the 'alleged murderer'. Yet every person he…no, she…had interviewed was convinced of his guilt. Was there really no one who even held doubts about his ability to commit this gruesome crime?

Asaf's neighbours had been keen to highlight his tendency to keep apart from them. He read the word 'loner' several times. Also 'kept himself to himself', 'scary eyes' and 'afraid of what he might do to me'.

Gidon's words were particularly sickening:

'There was always something strange about him. I knew very early on that something bad would happen if we kept him on. If it had been up to me alone, I'd have dismissed him long ago.'

Then the reporter, all without taking sides, cited cases of loners who had committed violent crimes after convincing themselves that this was the way out of their troubles, that everyone was against them and they had no choice but to take the law into their own hands. Only the previous week there had been such a case in America – Dallas. A man of twenty-eight, out of work and with no hope of improvement, had decided that his old school was responsible for all his current woes. He got hold of two guns – an easy task, it seemed, in America – smuggled them into the school, and started shooting random kids and teachers. Two teachers and six children had died. Others were injured.

Asaf felt extremely sorry for those who'd been involved and for the families affected, but the fact that he had been linked to these awful acts made him writhe with rage.

But it was Gidon, whose job it was to look after his employees and keep them motivated, who tipped Asaf's anger into fury. For three years, he'd come to work every day, sat at his desk while others drank coffee and gossiped, and designed and tested boards that had been manufactured and used in several different systems for various companies. And yet, when he was in trouble, no one stood up for him. No one at all. Not even the man who'd taken him on in the first place. They dismissed him as weird and were positive he was guilty.

Well, he would show them. He'd show them all.

Picking up the phone, Asaf dialled the number of the newspaper and asked to speak to Yonit Ramon, the journalist who had written the article. When he gave his name, he was put through immediately.

"I thought you were…"

"Locked up in police custody?" Asaf let his anger carry him through this ordeal. "They let me out. They realised I'm innocent. Aren't you people supposed to know these things?"

"We weren't planning another article about this until just before the trial."

"When your *loner* would be found guilty and the only unknown would be how many years, right?"

"I'm sorry. It did seem a pretty open-and-shut case. Tell me, could we meet somewhere, so you can tell me your side of the story?"

"Thanks to your article, I can't leave my flat, so you'd better come here if you want to talk to me. If you dare, that is. Oh, and bring some milk with you, please. I've run out, and I can't buy any more, because everyone has suddenly become scared of me."

As soon as Asaf ended the call, his phone rang.

"Asaf!" His mother shouted down the phone.

"Ima."

"So you're there. I knew all that stuff in the paper had to be wrong. How did they get your name and your picture? And what's all that about you being a loner?"

Asaf took a deep breath and blew it out slowly as if through a straw. A hysterical mother was definitely not what he needed just now. "I don't know, Ima. Must be a mistake. I'm trying to sort it out."

Relieved, she went on to relay all the gossip. First about his brother, then his sister, and lastly news of a few other family members. Asaf listened with half a mind. Throughout the conversation, a worrying thought attacked the other half. His parents, in Ashkelon, had a different newspaper delivered. They didn't read the free one he'd seen in town.

As soon as the call ended, Asaf took his laptop out of its drawer, rested it on his knees on the sofa and opened it up. A few short clicks confirmed what he'd suspected. His story was all over the national news. It included his name, his awful police picture, his apparent motive and his status as a loner, which clearly explained everything. His blood had reached boiling point by the time the journalist arrived at his door.

Strange how anger could override all Asaf's usual fears of people. For him, this Yonit woman represented everything that was wrong with society. She was all the people who had tried, committed and sentenced him because he wasn't like them. Therefore, there was no reason for Asaf to look up to her. On the contrary. He disdained her.

But she would be his communication tool. He would use her to tell his story.

"Can you tell me a bit about your background?" Yonit began. "How you became…"

"A loner?" Asaf emphasised the word.

Yonit nodded. And cringed. She sat on Asaf's sofa sporting her lipstick and her mascara and her long, stockinged legs, and looked down in embarrassment at the notebook perched on her raised knee.

Asaf, on the same sofa and twisted to face her, felt a bit of compassion coming on and forced it back. He had to concentrate on the anger part in order to get through this. "I've never told anyone about this before, but now that I've been exposed unwillingly, there's no point in trying to keep it secret any longer. I'm going to let you tell the world what it's like for me and…well, possibly for others like me. I don't know. I've never met any others, but I understand there are plenty out there. And you're going to print it because it's the least you can do after what you've caused me."

"I didn't accuse you. I only reported what other people said."

"And, by complete chance but, as it happens, in the same article, you followed what other people said with a summary of recent crimes committed by so-called loners."

Yonit opened her mouth, looking as if she was about to make excuses for her article. Then she seemed to change her mind. "Go ahead." She scribbled in the notepad, then looked up and waited.

"I was bullied at school. Not by one bully, not one group and not one year. It was all the way through. They all rejected me. Do you know what that does to you?"

Yonit shook her head.

"It destroys your self-esteem. It makes you think you're worthless. It made me hide away and stop talking to everyone, especially the people I looked up to – the ones I admired and those in a position of authority."

"Didn't the teachers help you?"

"The teachers? They're too busy dealing with the disruptive kids – the ones who stop them being able to get on with the lesson. If a child is silent, in their minds that's good. No need to do anything, except maybe to tell the parents, as if they have magic solutions. Parents don't study how to be parents, but teachers learn to be teachers. Yet, instead of using what they learn, they long for a simple life. They wish all the kids kept quiet."

"So, you're saying you didn't want to be a loner?"

"I don't think anyone wants to be a loner. It goes against the natural human instinct to socialise. I think people become loners because they think it's better than the alternative."

Asaf almost saw the wheels turning in Yonit's brain; turning her world conceptions upside down.
"What happened yesterday?"

"There's something I don't get," said Yonit, when Asaf had finished his tale. "You tell me you can't talk to people, but you've just told me this whole story, no problem."
"I don't know if I get it either, but… I read your article today. It was rubbish. It said loners live their lonely lives for years and years until suddenly they go out and kill someone, or they go on a rampage and kill a whole lot of innocent bystanders, because of some warped idea of revenge. And yes, I've also read about incidents like that, but those people are unusual. I think the world is full of so-called 'loners'. Most of them wouldn't dream of taking revenge on anyone and certainly wouldn't think of using violence. If they ever thought of ending a life, it would only be their own. What they want is for people to stop shunning them and help them integrate into society. And if journalists and others like you carry on making everyone think that all loners will turn violent, well, that's not going to be helpful to them, is it?"
"I guess not."
"In fact, it's going to ensure that they remain loners by making others afraid of them."
"I guess so."
"So I was angry. Furious. I still am. And I thought, as you've already probably ruined my life by exposing me like this, I might as well tell my story and at least use it to help others to be understood. Somehow, it was because I was angry that I was able to talk."
"Wow. I don't know whether to apologise for writing rubbish or to take credit for causing you to talk."
"When is this going to get published?"

"In tomorrow's paper, I expect. At a later stage, we might run an opinion piece on this story."

After Yonit left, Asaf returned to sit on the sofa and ruminate. As his anger dissipated, doubt and worry came to replace it. Had he been too harsh on the journalist, who was, after all, only doing her job? And how would his words come across to readers of the follow-up article? Would they understand his message, or would it make them even more antagonistic?

Chapter 20: Understanding Asaf

Left alone, Asaf thought back to his forced sojourn in the police station and remembered the chief inspector's words before his release.

"Have you heard of social anxiety?... I suggest you go home and look it up… Look it up and deal with it… Next time something even worse could happen to you…. Life's too short to spend it alone. It's other people who make life worth living."

Nadav had said something interesting, too. "It's good to have a name for your problem. It means you're not alone."

Asaf once again consulted his computer. When he put the words 'social anxiety' into his search engine, he gasped at the result. Over fifteen million hits.

He clicked one of them and read. Then he clicked another.

Before his eyes, appeared images of people who suffered just as he did. And as he read about their experiences, he pictured himself, and felt their pain through his…

Strangely enough, Asaf hadn't been good at Maths at school. Obviously, he improved because otherwise he'd never have acquired his engineering degree. But for most of his high school years, Maths remained the most annoying of his academic subjects. He'd have put it on a par with Sport, which he hated because of the team games. It wasn't clear to him, now, why he found Maths so difficult. It might have been the fact that he couldn't see the point of all the exercises they had to do. No one ever told them the many uses of Maths. It might also have been because of the teacher. He found her lessons particularly boring, and he hated it when she picked on him. Naturally, the other children loved it. They made sure to laugh at him when he gave a wrong answer and call him stupid, even though he excelled at almost every other subject.

It had been the same at university, every time a lecturer had asked Asaf a question. In the solitariness of his room, he could have answered easily, but with the lecturer and all the other students waiting for him to speak, he became confused and tongue-tied. He heard no laughter, but he felt its presence behind their eyes. Unlike at school, here he learned to push his fears about their opinions to the back of his mind as he concentrated on getting the work done. He heard the other students discussing problems together while he worked everything out by himself. It taught him independence, self-confidence and self-sufficiency. It helped him to find his own unique solutions, because he was never swayed by team members. He was free to try out his own ideas. But the lack of teamwork left him feeling lonely. Though confident about his work, he became increasingly depressed about his social abilities.

What did other people do about it? He clicked a few more links. There was a lot of talk about changing behaviour and changing thoughts; numerous articles by people offering to help. Clearly, there was no easy solution, and changing would require much hard work. It was all about taking risks.

He sighed. At present, it would be a risk to leave his flat, and not because of social anxiety.

Along with the milk, the journalist had brought him a variety of bourekas. It was a touching gesture as well as a life-saver. Asaf fetched the microwave from the top of his clothes cupboard, set it on the draining board and plugged it in. Then he stuck a few bourekas inside and soon sat down to savour the fillings – cheese, potato, mushrooms and spinach. One more meal and they'd be gone. Then what would he do?

One thing he didn't need to worry about was toilet paper. A full bag of it sat at the bottom of the wardrobe. Didn't anyone ever consider that thirty-two might be too large a number of rolls for a single man who never had visitors?

His phone rang again, this time from an unknown number. Who could it be?

The male voice sounded menacing. "You might have been released, but we all know you're guilty. And you'd better get away from this place before we decide to take the law into our own hands."

Asaf ended the call, but the voice continued to ring in his ears. The two remaining bourekas stayed on the plate. He felt sick to look at them. *The threat is empty*, said the logical part of his mind. *They would never do anything to me.* The rest of his mind was in turmoil. This was no electronics problem. This was a situation he couldn't handle alone. He needed help. Where would help come from?

He made himself repeat some of the words: "You'd better get away from this place." It sounded as if the man lived in this block. In fact, he probably got Asaf's mobile phone number via the house committee. He could even be on the committee.

Then he saw something appear under his door, reminding him that, increasingly anxious over his behaviour towards the departing journalist, he'd forgotten to put the door stopper in place. With shaking hands, he picked up the sheet of paper and unfolded it to find a hand-written note.

'You see, we know where you live. Leave this place quickly. Otherwise, you'll be leaving it wrapped in a shroud.'

Chapter 21: No Regrets

Nathalie found Yarden in the same position on the floor, still surrounded by her pages and folders. Thoughts of mentioning the downsides of remaining in the same awkward posture were overwritten by her need to divulge the revelation from Volodia.

"I found out something important, but I don't know if that brings me any nearer to solving the crime."

"You don't need to bother about solving the crime any more."

The tone of Yarden's voice was so nonchalant that Nathalie took a moment to realise her friend must have learned something important.

"What do you mean? Why not? He hasn't…"

"Your boyfriend has been released."

"He's not my b… What, really? That's fantastic." Still in her coat and boots, Nathalie dropped onto the rug beside Yarden and hugged her. "Yarden, that's wonderful. How do you know?"

"It's in the news: 'Loner released from police custody after being held for twenty-four hours.' You know how they write these things to make it sound as if the police have let a crazy lunatic go free."

Nathalie's elation deflated with the suddenness of a burst balloon. "Wow, I didn't think of that. They still think of him as a weird loner. People probably still think he's guilty. That doesn't sound good. Yarden, I need to talk to him. Can you find out his phone number?"

Asaf sounded distinctly aloof on the phone. But this wasn't the same as the shy aloofness she was used to. He even sounded angry. What did he think she'd done to him?

"Are you all right? Did they treat you properly?"

"Yes."

"Aren't you happy to be out?"

"I'm not sure yet. It seems I've swapped one cell for another."

"Why's that?"

"Outside, people recognise me as the murderer. They convicted me when they read that I was arrested. People scream when they see me. I've had terrible threats."

"*Mon dieu*!"

"I don't know what I'm going to do. I can't even leave my flat to buy food."

He still sounded angry. She didn't want to intrude, but clearly, he needed help from someone, and where would it come from if not from her?

"Could I bring you some food? What do you need?"

"I brought some other stuff, too," said Nathalie as she entered Asaf's flat. She purposely didn't mention the glares from two people who came down the stairs as she waited for Asaf to open the door.

What she could see of the place, at first glance, was immaculately tidy and rather sparse. Just the opposite of her cluttered shared apartment. But although the state of disarray made her cringe, it also felt homely and welcoming. This one looked sad and lonely. She knew she would never want to live on her own. "I thought… Could I make you a meal? I'm not a bad cook."

"I… Thank you."

The anger had disappeared, and with it the confidence that had helped Asaf to speak out on the phone. So it seemed to Nathalie.

He also looked awkward as he pushed the draft stopper into place with his foot, probably feeling her eyes on his back.

She looked around the tiny kitchen, wedged between the door and a room. "Do you have a dish that goes in the oven?"

Asaf didn't. It looked as if he hadn't even used the oven. But he had the dishes that came with the oven. They looked brand new. Nathalie decided to make a larger quantity of lasagne than she'd intended, to fit the dish. It could always be reheated later. Removing her coat, which Asaf put away in the cupboard, she busied herself preparing the sauce and the filling that, with the pasta, would make up the layers of the lasagne.

"It took a long time for the police to decide you were innocent, didn't it?"

"I… Yes."

There's more that he's not saying, thought Nathalie. *Something he's embarrassed about, maybe. I need to assure him I'm on his side.*

"I knew it from the beginning. I knew from working with you. The whole thing was ridiculous. I told that police chief that you couldn't possibly murder someone."

A look came into Asaf's eyes. Admiration? Kindness? The barrier was still firmly in place, preventing him from expressing his feelings in words.

"I've been trying to find out what really happened, so I checked out the people who work in the office and decided none of them could have done it. Then I discovered that the knife was part of the office equipment and had been bought by Ido. And there was someone else in the office – a stranger who was probably the murderer, but I don't know how to find out who the stranger was."

Again, Asaf broadcast awkwardness as he watched Nathalie work, standing by the entrance to what, she now realised, was the only room in the place. What she'd seen of the flat when she arrived was all there was.

"Why did you want to…?"

"They took you away. It was all wrong. I knew that. And then they kept you overnight. I kept thinking how awful that must be for you."

"I didn't sleep much in the cell. But it gave me time to think. When it all happened, I was in such a state of confusion, I didn't know what was going on. During the night, I kept trying to work it out. It's still all one big blur, but I have this feeling there was a movement behind me as I stood looking down at the body. Someone ran to the door. Someone with an uneven walk – a limp."

"That fits. He went down in the lift and ran out of the building very soon after you arrived. The guard saw him go. And yes, he had a limp."

"How do you know that?"

"I went to the office to talk to the guard – Volodia. It turns out… Well, I'll tell *you* this, but I don't want to tell the police. It turns out Ido bribed him to let the stranger in without getting his ID. Volodia's a new immigrant with all sorts of troubles. His father has dementia. He's scared of what they'll do to him, because there's no one else to look after his father." Did Asaf care about Volodia? Nathalie didn't know – only that she cared.

"Surely what Volodia did will come out in the end."

"That's why I advised him to call the police and tell them before they find out."

"And you did all this to help me? That's… Well, thank you."

Nathalie stopped sprinkling grated cheese over the dish and turned to look at Asaf. "You're worth it, Asaf. You're a good person. You were very patient with me in the office, explaining the job slowly and generally easing me into the work. Also, we get on well together and have a lot in common. And I felt it was only right to do what I could to help when you were in trouble. But then I got stuck. I didn't know how to find this anonymous man who ran out of the office."

Asaf shrugged. "But I'm just… It's my fault…"

"It's not your fault. Nothing is your fault. You're innocent."

"I did something stupid, getting hold of the knife like that. And then I didn't…couldn't explain everything to the police."

"Stop blaming yourself. Someone else caused all this." Nathalie put the dish in the oven. "Right, we've got three-quarters of an hour. Do you have something alcoholic to calm us down?"

"I don't drink much, but my parents gave me some sherry. They said it would be good for entertaining girls." Asaf tilted his head and looked down as he smiled. He found the bottle and two small glasses and poured drinks for them. Then he found a small packet of crisps and filled a little dish with them.

They sat beside each other on the sofa, not touching, the drinks and crisps on the bedside cabinet, which was now between them. The computer, at Nathalie's request, was open on the floor, playing Édith Piaf's *Non, Je Ne Regrette Rien*.

"I have no regrets? Is that what it means?" asked Asaf, helped by his knowledge of English.

"Yes. She says, 'I have no regrets about the past because my life begins today with you.'"

"That's sweet," said Asaf.

Nathalie wished she would be able to say the same words to Asaf, if not today, then soon. She surveyed the room. One sofa, one large cupboard and the cabinet-cum-table. Tidy, everything in its place, but lacking in character. The lighting was fairly good, considering that the only window was small and high up. Beyond the end wall was a raised storage area covered by sliding glass windows. This, she'd learned from visiting somewhere else, was called a *boydem* and was common in older apartments.

"I have two songs to play to you," said Asaf when the French song ended. "One is called *Hayom* and the other is called *Hayom, Hayom*. Do you know them?"

"When it comes to Israeli songs, I know nothing," said Nathalie.

"Then it's time you learned. There are some beautiful Israeli songs. And these two are both about how today is going to be different and better than all the days that came before. About life starting again from today. I sang them to myself yesterday morning on the bus to work. I did everything I could to get in the mood, to motivate myself to be proactive and make that day different from all the days in my life that went before."

"That makes sense." It didn't make complete sense to Nathalie, but she worried a question from her at this point might sound as if she doubted Asaf.

"And yesterday *was* different, but not in the way I intended."

"That wasn't your fault."

"No, but the way I reacted was my fault. If I'd handled the situation I found myself in as any normal person would, I wouldn't have been in so much trouble."

"I don't think there's a normal reaction to such an abnormal scene. You were in a state of shock, and that's perfectly normal. And anyone who's in a state of shock can do unexpected things. So, stop blaming yourself. I'll say it again: none of what happened yesterday was your fault."

"That's nice of you to say so…"

"Really, I mean it."

Asaf nodded. "Thank you, Nathalie. I'd be nowhere without your support."

"You need to believe in yourself. But everyone needs support and encouragement, sometimes."

"And help when they can't leave their apartment." Asaf's adjunct was tinged with sadness.

"Asaf," said Nathalie, "would you like to continue this investigation with me? I feel as if, now I've got this far, it would be nice to wrap it up and find the murderer."

"It would be. But what help can I be? I can't even go outside without someone recognising me and screaming."

"First of all, you have a computer and I bet you're a whizz at finding out information on it, especially as you understand Hebrew much better than me. Secondly, I asked my friend Tehila to go back to Ido's house and photograph some pages that might help. I'll see if she can send them, and then we can examine them together. Maybe they'll lead us somewhere. Thirdly, Tehila is studying acting and has learnt all about make-up and stuff. I bet she can change you so that no one recognises you."

"All right. Let's go for it."

Nathalie had never heard Asaf sound so excited. This, she thought, was the real Asaf, the one he kept under wraps, and she wanted more of it.

Even now, the real Asaf wasn't out the whole time. In fact, it was mostly hidden. But Nathalie caught glimpses of it trying to escape the covers. It showed in a grin, in a spontaneous remark, in a glance she hoped showed admiration for her. They progressed from aperitifs to the meal itself, still catching up on their knowledge of each other.

"This is very tasty," said Asaf, "but I expected you to make something French, not Italian."

"I'm prepared to accept that there are other cultures and cuisines, and lasagne seemed suitable for this evening, as I had the ingredients." Nathalie winked. Then she added, "How would you have managed without me?"

"I did have one more meal of bourekas left. That journalist brought them for me when I told her I couldn't leave the flat and didn't have any food. She brought the milk, too."

"That was nice of her. But…she brought you bourekas? Do you even like the things?"

"Actually, I do. Don't you?"

"They're okay, but they're nothing compared to croissants."

"Yeah? To me, both are tasty, but bourekas are more substantial. Croissants are just flaky pastry, but bourekas have great fillings."

"Each to their own taste," said Nathalie with a shrug. "Tell me about your childhood."

"I grew up in Ashkelon, the middle child of three. My older brother felt he had to assert his control over us. My little sister was always fighting for her place in the family. I gave in, every time. It made life simpler that way. Then there was school, where I got bullied, but I survived it."

Asaf smiled as if to say, Nathalie thought, *those bad things are in the past; life is better now.*

"Why… How did they bully you?"

"I don't remember how it started; it was always that way. And sometimes it was because I knew the consequences of saying something. I'd arrive at school on Sunday morning and all the kids would be talking about what they did on Saturday and who they did it with. You know, discos and parties and just hanging out. And I had nothing to say."

"But you did things, didn't you?"

"I did things on my own. I wandered around my city and didn't talk to a soul. If I'd told them about my weekend, they'd have laughed at me. So I kept quiet."

"That's sad."

"I wanted to be a part of what they did, but they never invited me, and I couldn't suggest it."

"Why not?"

"They'd have laughed at the idea."

In the quiet that followed, Nathalie decided Asaf had probably had enough of that topic.

"Has your family always lived in Ashkelon?"

"Oh yes. Even my grandparents lived in Ashkelon – all four of them. One of my grandfathers had a brother who died in the War of Independence. Apparently, he was very brave, and he died saving five other soldiers who were stuck in a tank. There's a square in Ashkelon that's named after him."

"Wow."

"All of our family were fighters in the army. My parents were disappointed that I wasn't. I applied, but they didn't accept me."

"Why not?"

"They said soldiers in fighting units have to work as a team and I was too much of a loner."

Nathalie thought about that. "You never know, when you decide to do something, what it's going to lead to. I mean, you basically kept away from your peers because of the bullies. You didn't know it was going to prevent you from going into a fighting unit in the army."

"That's true but… you know, you make your bed and you lie on it. Sometimes, the mattress isn't as comfortable as you meant it to be or the blanket leaves you feeling cold. Sometimes, you find yourself on a totally different bed and enclosed in the walls of a cell you can't escape from. Life can throw lemons at you, or oranges. You try your best to make life good, but in the end you have to take what you get, whatever it is."

"That's very profound. Well, I hope what you get in the future is better than what you've had up to now."

"Thanks. I hope you get what you want, too."

I hope we both want the same thing, thought Nathalie, but she asked something else. “What’s Ashkelon like? I’ve never been there.”

“It’s a town, on the coast. That’s what I liked about it. When I was old enough, I used to go off on my own to the beach, to swim and sit on the sand. I did a lot of walking. There’s the marina with the lighthouse at the end and the yachts in the bay. I used to watch people fishing, sitting there for hours, waiting for a bite. And there’s the big park up above with grass and trees and ancient structures. And great views. I used to sit, either up there or on the sand, and watch the beautiful orange sunsets.”

Asaf looked towards the bare white wall opposite. “One time next to the beach, there was a show going on. The circle was growing, and I pushed to the front to see and sat on the ground with the other kids. It was a magician. He was calling the kids up to take part and he pointed at me. I didn’t want to go, but he persuaded me. First, he asked me my name and whether I lived in Ashkelon. Then he asked where my parents were and was surprised to hear I came on my own. Then he asked me to pick a card from a pack. I chose one and it turned out to be the ace of diamonds, and he said I was a brilliant magician, then he gave me a prize. I didn’t think I deserved it, but everyone was clapping, so I took it.”

“What was the prize?”

“A furry toy dog. I loved it because the fur was so soft, but mostly because I’d won it.”

“Do you still have it?”

“My big brother was always jealous of me. He threw the toy in the bin and I never saw it again.”

Nathalie shook her head and bit her lip. Words seemed unnecessary. Then she thought back to Asaf’s description of his town.

“Is Ashkelon very old, then?”

"Ashkelon has been a city for thousands of years. It's even mentioned in the Bible. But now it looks modern. Only relics of previous civilisations still remain."

"I'd love to visit. Could you take me there and show me around?"

"Yes, if you want me to."

"I do. You know, I used to walk a lot in Strasbourg. There's no sea, but it has a big river, a medieval bridge and several medieval churches. There are whole areas where you walk into a different century. And theatre, opera, museums. A group of us used to meet up every weekend and…" She trailed off as her thoughts took over. For her, walking, activities, cultural events – they were all done with other people, never alone. She shouldn't have mentioned doing these things with others, but if she didn't, that would mean hiding who she was and everything in her past, and that couldn't be right either, could it?

"And what?" Asaf prompted.

Well, she'd started now. "We'd meet up and watch a play and then wander around or stop in a bar or a café. I do miss my city, but I know I can't live there any more."

"Why…why did you leave?"

"On Yom Kippur – the one before last – I was walking to the synagogue with my family when someone sprayed us with water and called us '*sales juifs*' – 'dirty Jews'. We weren't injured, but for me it was a wake-up call. You hear about incidents against Jews, but when something happens to you, the situation becomes more real. It wasn't an easy decision to leave my home town, but I made it and now I'm sure it was the right one."

"Well, I'm glad you made it. Otherwise I'd have been in a real mess, now. And hungry. I still don't understand why you're doing this for me, though."

"As soon as I heard they suspected you, I knew they were wrong and I was afraid you wouldn't stand up to them and tell them the truth. And I felt I had to find the real murderer so that you could go free. And now I'm this far away," Nathalie held her forefinger and thumb half a centimetre apart, "from finding him."

"But why did you believe in me when everyone else thinks I'm a murderer?"

"I know you better than they do. They all see you as…"

"A weird loner?"

"Well, yes, but I know you're not weird, you don't have to be a loner, and you're definitely no murderer. You know, when I was at university, my roommate was quiet like you. It was all about self-confidence. I used to tell her she had as much right to talk as everyone else, and things like that. She changed over the year, and I think I helped to give her the confidence she needed."

"You're a special person."

"Not really. I just try to help when I can."

As soon as the meal was over, Nathalie got busy. "Let's get on with the job. See what you can find out about Ido. I'll text Tehila to tell her to send me the photos and that we need her help with a disguise. Then I'll clear up the dirty dishes."

"I can do that," Asaf began. But seeing the logic in Nathalie's plan, he agreed.

After texting, Nathalie handed over her phone, so that Asaf could copy the photos she'd taken in Ido's apartment to the computer and examine them. While washing up, Nathalie heard a loud "Wow!" from the other room. She dried her hands and rushed to peer over Asaf's shoulder, screwing her eyes at a screen full of numbers and legal words.

"Ido Bitton changed his name in the Ministry of the Interior. His original name was Hanan Abutbul."

Nathalie tutted. “I can’t believe I missed that. Why did he change his name?”

“Probably because he didn’t want people in Jerusalem to know what he was up to when he lived in Be’er Sheva.”

“I thought he used to live in Lod.”

“He did. And before Lod, he lived in Be’er Sheva. Actually, it must have been in Lod that he changed his name.”

“Quite a nomad. What was he up to in Be’er Sheva?”

“Drug smuggling. He’d go off for so-called holidays abroad and return with the goods, concealed somehow.”

“How do you know?”

“He was suspected once, but they couldn’t nail him. I found a newspaper article about it.”

“So he moved away and changed his name and carried on with drugs?”

“I think he became a dealer. Seems he had to make money to support all those children.”

“And the new one on the way.”

“Right.”

Another screen popped up.

“What does this show?”

“These are the payments for two of the children. You can see why Ido needed money.”

“Yes. Wow. How did he find clients for the drugs?”

“I don’t know. But that’s what we need to look at next in order to get closer to finding the murderer.”

“Okay.” Nathalie sat close to Asaf on the sofa, in order to see the screen. A familiar warmth spread through her body as she found herself almost touching Asaf again. “How do we do that?”

“We could try searching for: how do drug dealers find their clients.”

"They wouldn't have information like that on public display, would they?"

"Let's see."

Well over two hundred million results flashed up. Nathalie gasped. Asaf started to click on the links.

"I think it's mostly through word of mouth. If you're in that world, you find people, or they find you. Even if you move from Be'er Sheva to Lod to Jerusalem, you're surrounded by druggies…junkies, whatever they're called, because you haven't left that world."

"How are we going to find Ido's clients?"

"I don't know."

"Tehila!"

"What?"

"I forgot to check if Tehila sent the photos."

Nathalie stood up and so did Asaf. In the process, his hand touched Nathalie's shoulder. He blushed and said, "Sorry," but Nathalie still wondered whether the gesture was completely involuntary.

Nathalie pressed on her phone. "They've arrived. Look, there's a long list of names and phone numbers. Can we look at them on your computer screen?"

With the details transferred, they peered at the screen. There was no indication of what the lists contained.

"Do you think they could be clients?" Nathalie asked.

"They could be, but they could also be suppliers. We'll have to be careful if we contact them. We don't want the suppliers to know we're on to them. And we don't want the clients to know either."

"So we have to pretend we're them. Suppliers. Or clients. Which?"

"Dealers. We're going to take over from Ido."

"Asaf, you're brilliant. Okay, there are two lists here. I guess the longer one is the clients."

"And one of those is the murderer."

"Right. We're getting closer. Isn't this exciting?"

"Oh yes."

The excitement, the adrenalin, their closeness, being totally in the moment. All these things combined to make their next action a natural consequence. They reached towards each other, opened their arms and hugged, their lips drawn together like cymbals, the resulting chime sounding only in Nathalie's head.

After a few seconds, they separated. "I'm sorry," Asaf began.

"No, don't apologise," said Nathalie. "That was perfect. Don't spoil it now."

Instead, Nathalie rested her head on Asaf's shoulder, and Asaf stroked her head, following her long, almost straight hair down to her shoulder.

After they broke away from each other, Nathalie made a series of phone calls. Each one began with a name check, followed by, "We're taking over your orders, starting with the customers who scheduled meetings for yesterday. Are you one of those?"

She went through the list, crossing off those who answered "No". When she'd finished, only one client remained on their list: Eran. There was no surname. Not knowing how these meetings were usually arranged, she thought it best to leave it up to him to decide on the time and place. He told her to bring the merchandise round to his house the following evening at ten. She told him there would be two of them, because she thought it might scare him if two people turned up when he was expecting one.

Chapter 22: Reminders of Home

Nathalie had gone back home to sleep, but she returned early, bringing frozen croissants with her for breakfast. Asaf insisted on having his cornflakes and milk first, but he agreed to try a croissant or two. The butter melted on the heated crescent-shaped, flaky roll.

Asaf seemed impressed. "This is tasty. You'll make a Frenchman of me yet," he joked.

Nathalie shook her head. "Not with this. But let's go to the Shuk later and get some real French food."

Asaf raised his eyebrows. "Your friend had better do a good job on me, first."

"I wish we could fast forward to this evening."

"Yes," Asaf agreed. "We're going to have to keep busy to avoid thinking about it all the time."

After breakfast, Tehila arrived in a temper. She hardly waited to be introduced to Asaf before launching into a tirade.

"Do you know what happened to me outside your door?" And as an afterthought, "Congratulations on being released, Asaf. You must be pleased to be home again."

"Not exactly—" began Asaf before Tehila interrupted him.

"Wait, you have to hear this. Remember I told you how some people react to me, Nathalie? Well, this was worse than ever. There were four people on the stairs out there and they all stared at me and shrank away, as if they thought I was going to attack them. I called to them, 'Haven't you ever seen a black person before?' and they didn't answer. I'm sick and tired of the racism in this country."

"Calm down, Tehila," said Nathalie.

"Calm down?" Tehila shouted. "I don't think you understand—"

"No, you don't understand. They didn't stare because of the colour of your skin. Someone stared at me when I arrived. It's because they think Asaf is a murderer, and I suppose they're suspicious of anyone who goes into his flat."

"But he was released."

"That doesn't come into it."

"Oh gosh, I'm sorry." Tehila's voice dropped several decibels. "I thought… I'm sorry for shouting. I thought it was me and I'd simply reached my limit for this week."

"Have a seat," Asaf ventured. He left the sofa for the girls and drew up the bedside cabinet for him to perch on.

Tehila chuckled. "It looks as if your seat serves many purposes."

Nathalie knew that her friend meant to calm the atmosphere and certainly wouldn't intentionally laugh at the sparseness or smallness of the flat. But she noticed straight away that Asaf blushed.

He'd closed up. His voice sounded forced and he looked hunched up and uncomfortable. Nathalie could account for the discomfort by what he was sitting on, and for the change in his voice by a nervous reaction to Tehila's outburst. Or it could be that the presence of a third person had caused him to return to being his usual, quiet self. Up until then, he'd been much more forthcoming than he'd ever been at the office, and that had pleased her.

Taking a deep breath, Tehila sat down and laid various makeup accessories on the sofa between her and Nathalie. "Look towards me," she said to Asaf. He'd been looking down and dutifully raised his vision to gaze at Tehila, but his serious expression and sad eyes revealed some of his inner thoughts.

Nathalie watched her friend as she turned Asaf into a different person. His hair was cropped with the lower part shaved, and then dyed black in the bathroom. A short matching beard was fitted on to look home-grown. Then a few brushes and some paint transformed his face, darkening his skin and eyebrows and lashes.

“That’s amazing,” she said, and Asaf agreed once he was allowed to look in a mirror.

“I’m glad I was able to help,” said Tehila, “and really sorry for the mix-up when I arrived.”

The three left together with no reaction, fright or otherwise, on the way. When Asaf and Nathalie parted from Tehila at the bus stop, she wished them good luck. Then, as Asaf had suggested, they walked to the Haas Promenade. The bright sunshine had caused Nathalie to agree to this, but the cold air meant that she was still glad of her boots and other accoutrements. To her, even the path of the Promenade looked special, built of Jerusalem stone and very light brown in colour, almost white. The same stone was used for the two inlets on the way, with stone seats and roofs.

After a while, a wooden bench in the sun welcomed them. They sat together looking down, past green and yellow trees and the beautiful purple-leaved bushes to the Dome of the Rock, the Church of the Ascension, the Hurva Synagogue, and all the other sites in the distance.

“This view is amazing,” said Nathalie, “and so close to where we live. How come I’ve never been here before?”

“Everything in this country is close,” said Asaf. “I’ve read that in the States you can travel for hours to visit one site. Israel is so tiny, you can see ten sites before lunch. It’s small and varied, full of history and modernity, snow and desert, seas and mountains."

Nathalie rested her head on Asaf's shoulder. She loved how excited he was about his country and looked forward to seeing more of it, hopefully with him.

"What sort of things did you like to do in France?" Asaf asked.

It was a normal sort of question, but Nathalie felt heartened by it. Asaf, she assumed, wouldn't have been used to asking such questions. He'd probably have been afraid, before, that people would think he was prying.

"I liked to walk, as you know. Apart from the exercise, when you walk you see the details of a city that you never spot when riding. You see boats in the river, the different types of people, and dogs, also out walking, you see all sorts of shops."

"That's true," said Asaf, and Nathalie was pleased he understood.

"Of the shows I went to, what I liked best was evenings out at the theatre. I miss that."

"Why don't you go to the Jerusalem Theatre?"

"I'm afraid I won't understand plays, here. Actors talk so fast, sometimes, I don't think I'd be able to follow."

"Oh, I bet you would. Your Hebrew's good. If we go together, I could explain anything you didn't understand. You should try it."

"I suppose you're right. If I never go, I'll never know."

"And you'll be missing out. They have some great plays on in the theatre."

From the Promenade, they walked back to the main Hebron Road and caught a bus to the Mahane Yehuda market, known as the Shuk, and Nathalie took Asaf straight along the main alleyway, bordered by stalls selling fruit, vegetables, meat and fish, to her favourite store – the one with a wide variety of delicious French cheeses. She even spoke to one of the servers in French. But then she reverted to Hebrew.

"Maurice, meet my friend, Asaf."

"Shalom, Asaf. I hope you take very good care of Nathalie. She is a very special woman."

"Oh yes. I know that." Asaf winked at Nathalie.

Nathalie picked out various cheeses, and Maurice gave Asaf several small portions to try.

"They're all delicious," he said. "But I'm not going to choose which to buy. You're the experts."

In the end, Nathalie chose four to take home. At a bread store, where she chatted to the seller in Hebrew this time, she bought a fresh baguette.

"It looks as if you've been here once or twice before." Asaf grinned.

"I miss my home country. This place helps to bring it back."

While there, they also bought fruit and vegetables before catching the bus back to Asaf's place.

"This will make a good lunch," said Nathalie on the ride home. "Another time, we'll buy white wine with a subtle taste, like Chardonnay. It completes this meal perfectly. But today, we need to keep sober and eat well before our ordeal, this evening." Then she covered her mouth with her hand. "I'm sorry, I shouldn't have reminded you."

"Don't worry," said Asaf. "It hasn't slipped my mind."

Chapter 23: The Forgotten Worker

After lunch, the winter light soon faded. They remained in the flat, trying to avert their minds from the evening rendezvous. A pack of cards helped for a while. And chatting.

"Nathalie. There's a song with that name, isn't there?"

"Ah, yes. It's beautiful and old, sung by Gilbert Bécaud. That Nathalie is Russian. She's his guide in Moscow. He goes back to her student room and she and her friends talk of serious things and laugh, as well. Then he returns to Paris, but he misses Nathalie, and he dreams of a time when she will visit him in Paris and he will be her guide."

"Nathalie, will you take me to France, one day, and be my guide?"

"I will. As long as you guide me in Ashkelon, and also help me to become a real Israeli."

"Does that mean you want to stay with me and be my girlfriend?"

"*Bien sûr*. Of course it does." She reached over and planted a kiss on Asaf's cheek. "It's like that other song. I have no regrets about the past because my life begins today with you."

Asaf kept her close with his arm. "*Hayom* – today we begin from the beginning. It's the same in every language." He turned to her, groaning breathily – a hint of internal struggle.

"Say it. Say whatever is on your mind."

"This feels like a dream. I can't believe it's happening."

"Asaf, I believe in you. You have to believe in yourself."

Asaf nodded. "I'm trying…trying to be someone I haven't been for an awfully long time."

"You're doing brilliantly," Nathalie insisted. "Maybe you need to make plans that would help. For instance, what are you going to do about work? Will you carry on working at Gidel?"

"After all the awful things they said about me? I think they'll have to manage without me. The new Asaf is going to look for a new job."

"Great," said Nathalie. "You should have done that ages ago."

"It might not have helped, ages ago. I needed something drastic to come and change me. Otherwise, the new job would have turned out exactly the same as the old one."

"This murder business has been fairly drastic."

"Yeah, this has been over the top, I'd say. Going out of your comfort zone doesn't usually mean flying to Mars."

Nathalie sniggered.

"Nevertheless, that's what I was planning on the day of the murder…the day before yesterday. It's hard to believe it was only two days ago. I decided I wasn't going to put up with being pushed to the side any longer. I had a few copies of my CV in my desk in the office, and I was going to give them to some other companies during my lunch hour. And I put a note in my pocket to remind me and force myself to go ahead. It said: 'Today will be different.'"

"Great."

"Not great. At the police station, they found the note and confronted me with it. They tried to get me to say it meant I planned to murder Ido."

"Oh no."

"But that ordeal is all over now, and I think it's changed me. I have a feeling I'm not going to be as overawed in my next interview as I was in the previous round."

"Great," said Nathalie again. "Although I'll miss working with you."

"We'll have to see much more of each other outside the office, then." Asaf's eyes had never seemed so bright, nor his expression so cheeky.

"Absolutely. We can walk together and go to the theatre together and…" Nathalie trailed off and frowned.

"What's up?"

"I just remembered. One of the pages we got from Tehila had a name on it that sounded vaguely familiar, but other things caught our attention and I forgot about it. I just remembered why I know that name, Arieh Salomon."

Asaf grinned. Nathalie was gesticulating again. "Who is he?"

"Don't you know? He comes into the office once a month to do the accounts. Everyone calls him Arik, so I didn't connect the name, at first. How could you not know him?"

"I knew someone came to do the accounts, but I never saw him."

Nathalie blinked her surprise. "Let's look at that page from Tehila again."

Asaf opened the laptop to see the page more clearly on the larger screen. "It looks as though Ido has been getting regular sums from Gidel via this guy, Arieh."

"For how long?"

Asaf calculated. "Seven months. The amount increased, last time."

"I need to talk to him."

"I don't know how to get his phone number."

"Yarden is good at that. Or else, I can message him via Facebook. I'll try that."

Arik replied to Nathalie's text immediately. He suggested meeting in a restaurant in the town centre.

"I'll go with you," said Asaf. "I don't like you doing these things alone."

"I can manage." Nathalie raised her voice, peeved at Asaf's wish to protect her.

"I'm sure you can," Asaf rushed to assure her. "But I'm involved in all this. I want to be part of it."

"Asaf, I'm sorry, but I think I should do this alone. I need him to open up and I think he'll be more afraid if he sees two people."

"All right. But text me as soon as you can, after the meeting."

"I will." Despite her initial irritation at Asaf's suggestion that she couldn't manage on her own, Nathalie found his worry about her safety touching.

***

Again, Mazal lowered herself into her chair by the window. The garden, still visible in the fading light, stood empty of humans. Birds flew around searching for a bed for the night, watched keenly by a dark brown cat.

"Shall I turn the light off?" Shmuel asked.

"No, I don't think there'll be anything to see today."

"Strange, what happened yesterday." Shmuel came over to the window and stood beside his wife.

"Yes. I keep thinking maybe we should have called the police."

"It's not too late to do it now. And you're right. It could be something important. They wouldn't let on who called them, would they?"

***

Tmol Shilshom stood in Nachalat Shiva, a quaint neighbourhood full of old buildings with arches and hidden niches, linked by twisting alleyways. Inside the restaurant, the walls and floor were made of tiled stones and the floor dipped in places. The windows and doors were arched, and books stood on wooden shelves. The dark wooden tables and chairs added to the atmosphere, while the computer screen on the counter in the corner looked as out of place as a car in a novel set in the twelfth century. Nathalie smiled when she reached the place, glad that Arik had chosen to meet in this reminder of a previous era that was a favourite of hers.

They'd arranged to meet outside, and Arik soon turned up. She recognised his tall, slim frame and clean-shaven, youngish face. But today, it came without the usual happy grin. In fact, Nathalie observed, his face was lined with worry. He was hiding something, she thought. But would he tell it to her?

His hand reached upwards, indicating that she should climb the stairs first. At the top, she turned into the room on the left and found a free table for them. They both took off their outdoor garments and hung them over their chairs. Arik looked good in dark blue jeans and a striped navy and burgundy long-sleeved top. They sat facing each other, a stone wall on one side, customers and staff walking past on the other. Nathalie had prepared a topic for small talk, but Arik launched straight into business.

"So, you're doing some investigating into this murder."

Nathalie raised her eyebrows. "How did you hear that?"

"From Gidon. He thinks it's dangerous and you should leave that job to the police."

"I want to clear Asaf's name. Even though the police released him, people still think he's guilty. If I can find the murderer, then they'll know he's innocent."

"What if he really is guilty?"

"He isn't."

Arik opened out the palms of his hands, looking unconvinced. Nathalie could have explained why she was so sure of Asaf's innocence, but she wanted to follow a different tack.

"Why was Ido blackmailing you?" She watched Arik's eyes open wide in shock.

"Why do you think that?"

"I saw a page that Ido kept locked up. It showed regular amounts he'd received from Gidel but through you."

Arik sat hunched over the table, both elbows on it. The top of his head rested on one palm. The other hand rubbed his chin. She'd noticed that gesture from him when they first met. It looked to her as if he was stroking an imaginary beard. Perhaps he used to have one.

The waitress startled them out of a reverie. They both ordered herbal teas. Nathalie knew the food in this place was delicious, but this wasn't the time to enjoy it.

The waitress went away but Nathalie kept watching Arik. He looked uncomfortable. He averted his eyes from her and wiped sweat from his forehead. Finally, seeming to have reached a decision, he looked back at Nathalie and spoke.

"I used to be haredi."

Nathalie opened her mouth. She certainly wasn't expecting that. She tried to imagine Arik dressed in a black suit with tassels hanging out. The beard she'd wondered about before grew longer in her mind and was bordered by sidelocks that flopped down from above. On his head sat a big black hat. Yes, that could work.

Arik continued. "I didn't learn anything secular, not even at school. After school, I spent my days in a yeshiva, studying the religious books." He rolled his eyes. "The only useful thing I learned from the rabbis there was how to learn. But it became my job to keep the accounts for the yeshiva. I learned the job from experience; I never earned any qualification. When I left and became secular, I found myself in trouble. I needed money fast and bookkeeping was the only secular profession I knew. But I'd never studied it and…well, I ended up faking my certificate in order to get work. I know it was wrong, but I was desperate.

"Then I met my wife to be and now we have two children. I needed to keep working, and still do. My wife doesn't know I didn't earn my certificate."

"Aren't there organisations that help those who leave the haredi community?"

"I didn't know about them, then. I was destitute, sleeping on the streets, and desperate to get out of that situation. I thought I had no choice."

"How did Ido find out?"

Arik sighed. "He must have guessed somehow. Then one day, he invited me for a drink in the Irish Pub on the way home from work. He was… Well, you know how charming he could be. I didn't suspect a thing. I only had a couple of drinks that day, but I suppose it was enough to make me less wary. I told him. I boasted how I'd managed to fool all the companies I worked for. I asked him not to tell anyone. I can't believe I was so stupid." He covered his face with both hands.

"Erm, Arik, the waitress wants to put your tea on the table."

With a jerk, Arik removed his arms from the surface, his cheeks reddening. He waited for the waitress to leave before continuing.

"Ido got me to fiddle the accounts at Gidel in return for keeping my secret. He insisted on getting a regular sum, each month. I had no choice. Then, last time, he wanted it increased. I was worried someone would find out in the end. When it's small sums, the bosses don't notice, but larger sums are much trickier." Arik took a sip of his mint tea. "You won't tell this to the police, will you? I don't know what I'll do if this comes out."

"That depends."

The lines on Arik's face grew deeper. "What do you mean?"

"Ido was blackmailing you. Last time, he forced you to make the amount higher. No doubt, he would have continued to raise the stakes, and make it more and more dangerous for you. But fortunately, he's no longer around because someone removed him from the scene."

Arik's face had grown dark. His eyes had shrunk to slits. His hands, resting on the table, clenched into fists.

"Are you suggesting I murdered him?" His voice sounded forced. He seemed to be struggling to control it.

"It's a possibility. I'm not sure." Nathalie's voice sounded more hesitant than she'd intended. Her heart was beating fast. Was Arik the murderer? The grey straggly hair and beard could have been false. The limp could have been acted. And if he was, she could be in grave danger at this very moment.

Still clenching his fists, and with the same forced, threatening voice, Arik said, "I think we should continue this conversation outside."

"I think not," said Nathalie, her heart still thumping at double time.

Arik jumped up from his chair, grabbed the jacket he'd hung on the back and stormed out of the restaurant.

Nathalie reached for her phone and texted Asaf, not trusting her voice enough to phone him. In just one minute, he was by her side. She jumped up and threw her arms around him. When she let go, tears were streaming down her cheeks. She sat down and reached into her bag for a tissue. Asaf sat opposite her, on the chair so recently vacated by Arik.

Asaf waited for Nathalie to calm down before asking, "What happened?"

"He became furious at the suggestion that he could have murdered Ido. I'm sure that, in a different place, he would have strangled me. I've never been so frightened."

"I shouldn't have let you meet him alone."

"It was all right. He couldn't really do anything to me in here. But what were you doing? How did you get here so quickly?"

"I was worried about you, but you didn't want me to go with you. So I caught the next bus into town and waited downstairs. Then I saw a man who could have been Arik carrying a jacket. He ran down the stairs and marched straight to Jaffa Road. Must have been in a hurry."

"Or extremely angry. He wanted me to go outside with him. I refused. Then he just left, without a word."

"Sorry if I got in your way."

Nathalie shook her head. "I'm really glad you were there. I've never been so scared in my life."

"That's getting to be a habit – people leaving you without saying anything."

Nathalie rolled her eyes. Yes, she'd told Asaf about Omer's strange behaviour in the park. "I wish it was because of my personality, but I fear it's more sinister."

On the table, Asaf placed his hands on top of Nathalie's. They felt large, warm and protective. "I'm not leaving you again until this is over. I don't care what you say."

Coming from anyone else, that remark might have annoyed her. But it came from Asaf, and it pleased her to see this other, assertive side of him.

On the way home, they picked up a free newspaper and Nathalie stuffed it into her bag.

Chapter 24: Hiding the Evidence

Sunday

He drew a hand across his aching head and blinked to focus his eyes. The living room came into view, though still obscure. He blinked again and winced at the random objects strewn all over the dusty floor. A towel, a shaver, a sweater, a book, loose pages torn from a folder in a fit of frustration, a needle, a coat. Iris would have hated the mess. So would he…once.

Memory flashed over him. He'd thrown down the coat and picked up a blanket before falling asleep on the sofa. It had been daytime. Day, night – what did it matter? It was all the same to him.

Once, it was important. They had a schedule, he and Iris. Getting up, breakfast, the short walk to the campus. They did it all together, every day, for thirty years. Children weren't to be, but they had each other. It was all they needed.

He was the poet, but she, the historian, was the one who discovered that Shelley's wife kept Percy's heart for thirty years. "Let's do that," she said. Her eyes lit up with inspiration. She was so beautiful, so perfect. "Whoever is left will keep the other one's heart in a drawer of their desk. Then we'll never be apart. Okay?"

It was easy to talk of dying when they were young and that prospect was – had to be – a long way into the future. Without hesitation, he agreed to her request, never imagining that he would be the one left behind, or that it would come to pass so soon.

They didn't let him keep the heart. It didn't fit Jewish tradition, they said. Instead, he used a brooch he'd given her for an anniversary. Surely, that was in the tradition, like all the symbols of the first night of Passover – the blend of apple, cinnamon and wine called charoseth symbolising mortar, wine for blood, and so on. He and Iris weren't religious, but they'd continued the tradition of the seder night, often celebrating with Guy and his family. Their parents had unfortunately died too soon, but that had made the brothers more aware of the importance of family and keeping close.

The brooch was made of silver and in the shape of a heart. She'd kissed him and thanked him when he presented it to her, and he'd drawn her in close for a hug. Now, it lived in a transparent plastic box in the top drawer of his desk, in a corner of the living room. The box had a rectangular cross-section, like a coffin. He often opened the drawer and talked to it, but she never responded, probably angry that it wasn't her real heart. "I did what I could," he wailed to her. *But answer came there none.* And when he thought of those words, he wept again. For relaxation, they often used to read nonsense rhymes together, and *The Walrus and the Carpenter* was one of Iris's favourites.

There, on the shelf, surrounded by books, stood a small picture frame holding a photo of Iris. It was her favourite, taken in the Hula Valley in spring, when irises were in bloom. She loved the bright yellow ones the best. Standing beside them, in brilliant sunshine, she radiated happiness and perfection.

He shivered and rubbed his hands together, then tried to warm them on the radiator. No, of course, the heating oil had run out. But the coat would help. He picked it up and gasped. The front of the long, dark grey coat was covered in stains that could only be blood. Or wine? No. He was truly shocked. He let go of the coat and went to sit on the sofa.

Then the events of that morning came flooding back to him. It all happened so quickly. He hadn't intended to do what he did.

Still on the sofa, he shivered and sobbed. Big tears fell on his jeans. Who cared? He was a murderer, and had to face up to that. It changed everything. Now, he was definitely on the wrong side of the law – no longer any doubt. He had to start thinking like a criminal, to hide all evidence. And the first thing he had to do was to bury that coat, as soon as darkness descended.

A pang of hunger propelled him to the fridge. Its emptiness extended the pang to heartbreak. It was never empty when…

He took out a crust of bread and the remainder of the cottage cheese. It would stave off the hunger, but it wouldn't help the heartbreak, caused by loneliness and grieving, which was why he'd turned to drugs in the first place. Only dope could assuage that pain.

Fetching a plate and a knife was pointless. Who would see him? Dipping the crust in the cottage cheese, he tore off a bit with his teeth. The dope had led to the university dumping him. He hadn't always turned up to lectures. They warned him, then they let him go. He understood.

The next bite almost finished the crust and the cottage cheese. He was going to need more food. There was no money in his bank account. What about his wallet? Fishing it out of his pocket, he examined the contents. One shekel and sixty agorot. That wouldn't buy him one little bread roll. Nothing for it.

On his phone, he chose the well-clicked number marked 'Guy' and heard a resigned "Hello." Once, they'd enjoyed keeping up to date with each other. Now, he'd become a burden to his younger brother.

"Do you think you could…" His voice tailed off.

"Again?" Anger came from Guy's voice. He cringed but kept the phone to his ear. "Listen, I'll put money in your account now and that has to be the last time. I have a wife and kids to think of and you have to get help. You can't carry on like that. I mean – really – you're a psychologist. If you don't know what you have to do to put yourself right, I don't know who does."

Too late, he thought, closing the call. *Too fucking late.*

Darkness arrived. He found an old jacket in the cupboard, and a large torch, which he checked, glad to see the battery still worked. Out in the little garden, clutching the coat, he retrieved the spade from the shed and walked down past the lemon tree. Iris loved that lemon tree. She marvelled at the flowers that bedecked the tree each spring, and went out every day to see how much the fruit had grown. Every day until she couldn't any longer. Then he took over, continuing to care for the tree and keep it watered for her.

His leg hurt. It always hurt, a constant reminder of his big failure.

As he began digging, somewhere above a light turned off, throwing him and his growing pit into darkness. He swivelled the torch to shine directly on him. Memories of a previous dig pleased and haunted him. Aged sixteen, he joined a summer excavation. It was fun and exciting. As well as a pot or two, he found the love of his life, Iris, while digging in the sun.

Now, there was no sun and no Iris. Just the light from the torch and a cold, biting wind. He flicked his hair behind his shoulder, but it kept coming back, blocking his eyes.

When the pit was big enough, he tossed the coat in and covered it up, doing his best to make it look as usual. Now that he'd completed this task, he could reward himself.

Chapter 25: Ex-loner

Between the entrance and his front door, a young man jumped out at him. Asaf recognised him from the flat beside his, although they hadn't spoken.

"Ha! Caught you," shouted the neighbour. "I know it's you, even if you do look different. I warned you to go away. This is a respectable block. It's not a place for criminals like you."

The man got hold of Asaf's neck and tried to push him down to the floor, but Asaf slammed his fist at him, winding him and causing him to loosen his grip. Asaf pulled the hands off his neck, pushed him down and held him there.

"I'm not a criminal," he said firmly. "The police made a mistake. When they realised it, they let me go. However, if you get arrested for attacking me, that won't be a mistake. Is that what you want? Do you want my girlfriend to call the police now?"

The neighbour shook his head.

"Will you leave me alone now?"

The man nodded.

"You'd better." As soon as Asaf released his grip on him, he retreated into his flat.

Nathalie, who'd been watching from a safe distance, moved closer to give Asaf a hug. "I'm proud of you. You stood up to him."

"I'm glad to hear that. I was worried you'd think I was too violent."

"No. He started it and he deserved what he got. And you also explained the truth to him. It shows a belief in yourself that wasn't there before."

Back in the flat, Nathalie pulled out the newspaper, then gave a squeal of excitement. "Asaf, it's you on the front page."

"That's right."

"You knew. Why didn't you tell me before?"

"In the centre of town? I didn't want strangers realising it was me."

Nathalie read the first paragraph, despite struggling with some of the words. "When you said you talked to the journalist, I didn't imagine you'd said all this."

"I still don't know how I managed to do it." Asaf joined Nathalie on the sofa.

"It looks like an excellent article. Listen to this.

"Asaf Levitt, who was arrested on Sunday for the murder of Ido Bitton in the office of Gidel Electronics in Har Hotzvim, Jerusalem, was released on Monday and all charges against him were dropped. The police spokesman who announced this said the investigation into the murder was continuing and declined to comment further.

Gidon Regev, CEO of Gidel Electronics, who described Levitt as 'strange' on Sunday, declined to comment on the release.

Levitt himself expressed anger at the article that appeared in Monday's edition announcing his arrest. In particular, he took issue with the linking of his case to previous crimes committed by people who live apart from society."

Asaf pulled the paper from her to rest it on his lap and read quickly and fluently, despite his increasingly flushed face.

"'There are a lot more loners than you think,' Levitt said. 'You don't notice them because they try to keep out of the way. They don't go around with shirts that say: 'Keep away from me, I'm a loner.' And most loners don't consider revenge at all, let alone violent revenge. But you don't hear about them. You only hear about the very small minority who get noticed by doing something terrible, so you assume all loners end up committing crimes like that.'

Levitt claimed the article had led to an assumption of guilt by his neighbours, making it impossible for him to leave his apartment. However, he also admitted that they probably hadn't held him in high regard beforehand. 'I didn't want to shun them,' he added, 'but I didn't know how to connect with them and they certainly didn't reach out to me.'"

Nathalie had been trying to follow the newspaper text while Asaf read it aloud. Now, she looked up and tried to interpret the expression on Asaf's face. It was one that couldn't make up its mind whether to show pleasure or embarrassment. "What made you talk to her?"

"I was so angry with what she'd written, I decided I had to tell her the truth. There's a lot more that I said. I think it's going to appear later as an opinion piece."

"You told it very well. I think it's the best thing, really. It's no good keeping it all inside. No one can be understood if they don't talk."

"That's true. But it's scary. I feel as if I've been carved open and crowds are going to stream past staring at my insides."

Nathalie raised her eyebrows. "As long as that remains metaphorical, perhaps opening up is the best way. It's what you didn't do, as a child." She looked up at the ceiling and back to

Asaf. “Actually, why didn’t you tell your parents about the bullying at the time?”

“I tried once and it didn’t help, so I didn’t bother after that. My parents were stressed enough, as it was. I felt my goal in life should be not to be a bother like my brother and sister.”

“It’s amazing how some young children can sense the difficulties the adults close to them are going through, and end up caring for them.”

“That’s true. I knew instinctively that I had to protect them from having to worry about me, too.”

“But now you’re free to live your life as you want. And it seems you want to become an advocate for loners.”

“Yes, I feel quite passionate about that. I can speak for loners because I used to be one. And because I got my voice back.”

“You used to be a loner, but you are no longer?”

“Absolutely. You’ve seen to that, and I can’t thank you enough.”

Chapter 26: What Really Happened

Monday

Eran took his phone out of his pocket. He shivered. The old ragged jacket wasn't enough to keep him warm. The winter coat might have been… Oh yeah, he got rid of it, yesterday. Either yesterday or the day before. The dope had felt amazing before it knocked him out.

Actually, burying the coat in the garden probably wasn't the best idea. In fact, it was downright stupid. If he ever became a suspect, they'd easily find it. He sighed. It wasn't as if it was heavy, like a body. It was just a coat. He could have taken it far away from here. Then they wouldn't have linked it to him. Silly that, but too late now. If he dug it up, someone might see. Better to leave it now and hope for the best.

He removed a worn glove to choose the number at the top of his contacts, then put it back on his icy hand.

The call was answered, but no one spoke. Eran heard breathing from down the line. "Guy…"

"Yeah."

"Thanks for the money."

"You're welcome."

"It won't last long. Then what can I do?"

"I don't know. Get help. You can't carry on like this."

"Couldn't you make it a little more?"

"I can't do it any more, Ran. Can't bail you out. I'm sorry."

"Please. I'm desperate."

Eran heard a loud sigh. "Leora's pregnant again. We need to save up for a bigger place. I can't keep supporting my older brother. I just can't."

"How am I going to manage, Guy?"

"Stop making me feel guilty. There's nothing more I can do. I'm sorry. I've got my own family to think of. I wish it could be different, I really do. I'm so sorry, Ran, but that's how it is."

The phone went dead. Eran dropped onto a chair and covered his face with his hands. Now even Guy wouldn't help. Things were going from bad to worse. What could get him out of this mess?

He opened the top drawer and took out the box with the heart brooch. "Iris, what shall I do, please answer me." But she didn't. How could she? It wasn't her real heart. He'd failed to get her heart as he'd failed in everything since her death.

Even his suicide failed. He'd jumped off a high building only to land on a passing lorry and damage his leg. They tried to tell him life was worth living. It wasn't, of course, but he didn't want to disappoint them, so he thanked them for saving his life while secretly wishing they hadn't.

When he came back from the hospital, he'd looked for ways to mask his grief. The substances became stronger as their effect weakened. Always, their power was only transitory.

Eran opened another drawer and reached to the back of it for the syringe and the portion. Only enough left for one time. Why didn't he have more of it? Yesterday, yesterday morning, early, he'd gone to get more. He'd followed instructions, going into the office building and past the desk to the lift. He was ready to give a name to the guard and sign in, but the guard looked away, as if he purposely didn't want to see. He'd taken the lift up and walked along to the office called Gidel, as instructed.

Eran knocked and the guy he called Shalom – his dealer – opened the door immediately and let him in. Eran remembered the conversation.

"I've come for the stuff."

"I'll give it to you when you give me the money."

"I haven't got it now, but I'll get it for you."

"That's not good enough. I need the money now. No money, no fix."

So it had gone on, back and forth. Eran's desperation forced him to beg.

"Please, I'll get the money, I promise you."

'Shalom' had shaken his head and put his hand back on the handle of the door, ready to unlock it with the key in his other hand, then pull it open and push Eran out.

Eran couldn't let that happen. He needed the stuff more than anything. "No!" He got hold of Shalom and threw him across the room. Shalom fell flat on the floor, and that's when Eran saw the knife in his hand. In a flash, he held Shalom down with his foot and forced the knife from him. Then there was a sudden sharp pain from his leg, the one that was meant to be keeping Shalom flat on his back. Why did that damned excuse for a supporting limb always fail him at the worst of times? He must have stopped pressing, enabling Shalom to slide out and stand up. Still gripping the knife, he turned to face Shalom, who charged at him, and the knife ended up in Shalom's body. Eran hadn't meant to do it. It had been totally unplanned. All he'd wanted was to get his dope. If Shalom had only given it to him…

Before escaping, he had to find the stuff. He'd begun to search Shalom's pockets when he heard the sound of a key turning in the lock. Instantly, he jumped back and crouched down behind the long lobby desk.

Someone came in and closed the door. Peeping round the edge of the desk, Eran saw a man swivel round to a small cupboard on the wall. He heard him make a surprised "Oh" and saw him turn towards the middle of the lobby. He heard the man gasp when he spotted the body, then watched him go over to it and stand there looking at it, completely still, his back to the route from the desk to the door. Without a sound, Eran manoeuvred into a runner's sprinting position. After a moment, he took his chance and slipped out, moving as quickly and as quietly as his gammy leg would allow.

Eran had taken the lift down, and kept his head lowered. No one tried to stop him. There were a few stares from passers-by on the now crowded street. They weren't used to seeing people who looked the way he did in the technological park. He'd kept going.

Today, Eran had ventured out to the grocer shop for some bread, milk and cottage cheese, which the shopkeeper agreed to put on his account, and he picked up the free newspaper. Someone else had been arrested, suspected of committing the crime. Must have been the guy who came in – the one he saw. There was a chance he'd get away with it.

Shivering on the sofa, Eran covered his face with his hands. What had happened to him? Someone else might be sent to prison for a crime he'd committed – a murder, no less – and he felt relieved, pleased even. What a terrible person he'd become. No wonder Iris would never answer him.

Eran was about to put his last fix into the syringe when his phone rang. Must be Guy to say he'd changed his mind and would help him after all. His kind little brother always came to the rescue in the end. He put the stuff down and picked up the phone.

It wasn't Guy or anyone he recognised. It was a woman. She sounded quite young, but you could never tell with women. She spoke with a French accent. "We're taking over your orders, starting with the customers who scheduled meetings for yesterday. Are you one of those?"

At the end of the conversation, Eran closed the call. Then he put the syringe and stuff back in the drawer. This was no time to get high. He needed to have his wits about him now and plan this properly. He needed to practise, too.

Closing all the blinds to avoid any nosy neighbours, he headed to the kitchen to find the long carving knife – the one with the sharp point and edge. He also retrieved the knife sharpener from the back of the cupboard.

Chapter 27: Keeping the Appointment

Back at Asaf's place, they still had a couple of hours to kill before their evening appointment. Nathalie tried to look past it.

"Tomorrow, if the weather's fine, lets walk along the path from the First Station to the zoo."

"Sounds like a good idea," said Asaf, "if…"

"If what?"

"If nothing. Let's leave it at that."

Nathalie nodded. She knew perfectly what he meant.

Leaving soon after nine, they took two buses to the French Hill neighbourhood. On the way, Nathalie said, "This morning, I wanted to make time go faster so that we didn't have to wait so long for this. But now, I'm glad we had all those hours to get to know each other better beforehand."

"I agree," said Asaf. "And you also got to talk to Arik."

"That's true. Although nothing really came of it, and he might still turn out to be the murderer."

They found the address Eran had given them. Inside the building, they climbed one flight to reach Eran's flat. Like many blocks in Jerusalem, this one was built on a hill, its back higher than its front. Nathalie rang the bell and they waited for about a minute. Then the door opened slowly. They entered together.

"Hello," Nathalie called. "Is anyone here?"

Suddenly, the door slammed shut behind them. Before she could turn, Nathalie was pushed so hard that she toppled over, only just managing to put her hands out to prevent her head from crashing on the hard tiles. By the time she raised her head and turned it, Asaf was lying beside her, his hands tied behind his back with what looked like white zip tie. Crouching on top of him was a man with long, grey, straggly hair and beard.

"Don't move," shouted the man.

Nathalie felt a knee on her back, too, making movement almost impossible, in any case, especially after her hands were tied like Asaf's. Following the man with her eyes, she saw him reach over and pick up a long knife that he held against Asaf's neck. He placed his free hand on Nathalie's neck squeezing it with his thumb and middle finger, or so it felt.

This time, Asaf wasn't the only one who was tongue-tied. Nathalie was, too. Eran, on the other hand, had plenty to say.

"Nice little trick I learned in the army," he said. "You weren't quite expecting this, were you? Thought you were so clever, solving the murder all by your little selves, right? Well, let me tell you: you don't know anything. You don't even know that a dealer would never go to a client's home."

"Oh, so you knew straight away that we weren't who we said we were."

Amazingly, that came from Asaf. What had enabled him to speak? Nathalie was still unable to.

"Yes, I knew all right, and you gave me plenty of time to get ready. A whole day. You were asking for it."

"I suppose we were. We didn't realise."

Nathalie watched the glint of the knife on Asaf's neck. How could he speak at a time like this?

"It's the ABC of being a dealer. You have to keep open the element of surprise for your own safety. You tell the client the place and time at the last minute. Oh my god. A couple of little innocents, you are."

"You were fortunate, then, that you had this knife and the zip ties."

"It's just a kitchen knife, sharpened extra fine. The zip ties were a memento from the army. I imagined using them to tie parcels. Good thing I never did."

Nathalie lay frozen on the cold, hard tiles, hardly believing this conversation was really going on. Yet, Asaf continued to ask questions.

"How did this all start? What were you doing in our office?"

"The guy you call Ido, he was my dealer. He told me to go to the office early in the morning to collect my next delivery."

"This is what I don't get. If he told you to come to collect it, why did you have to kill him?"

"That was a mistake. We argued over money. He threatened me with a knife. Probably didn't know I learned to use a knife in the army."

"Yeah, but he had the knife, not you."

"I got it off him. It's not hard when you know how. It's been a long time, but we trained well. You don't forget a thing like that."

"No, I suppose you don't. But why did you need to kill him?"

"I told you, it was a mistake. The idiot charged at me when I was holding the knife. It all happened so quickly. I didn't have time to think."

"Yeah, I see that now. Tell me about the trick – the one you used on us. How does it work?"

"Exactly what you saw. I open the door and stand behind it. You walk in. I slam the door shut. Before you can turn round, I push you down and nail you there, tying your hands."

"You make it sound easy, but I bet it's hard to pull off. You must have practised a lot."

"Fortunately, you let me have plenty of time to practise." Eran shifted his position and concentrated his attention on the knife and their necks.

Was he preparing for the next stage of the exercise? Asaf seemed to have run out of things to say. Natalie knew she should take over, but she couldn't.

Just then, the door flung open, and Nathalie felt the weight on her back removed and with it the knife. There were two clicks, which could have been handcuffs, and a familiar voice said, "Take him away."

Then that familiar voice acquired a strange accent. "*Oh là là!* Nathalie, we meet again. What luck!"

That was one thing she hated about this country: the way people thought it was fine to try to imitate her accent.

But this time, it enabled her to find her voice. Asaf was right. Anger could free the vocal cords. "Hello, Barak."

Did the police chief have to peer down at her from that great height?

Someone squatted down, freeing their hands with wire cutters, but Barak continued to tower over them.

"And here's someone else I know, looking slightly different. Am I right, Asaf? Oh sorry, I forgot. You don't talk to me, do you? Nathalie, I'll try you. What do you have to say for yourselves?"

"I'm sorry, Barak. We thought we could solve the whole crime and then no one would suspect Asaf any longer."

"You're lucky *we* solved it when we did, thanks to one of the neighbours who saw Eran burying something in the garden. We dug up a blood-stained coat this evening, and then put a guard on this place while we continued to investigate. The guard saw you go in. Fortunately, I was close by. Otherwise, I'd have been dealing with a triple murder."

There was nothing else to say, so they didn't.

"If he'd had his senses about him, he wouldn't have buried his coat in the garden. He'd have tossed it in a bin far away from here and we'd have been none the wiser. Then where would you have been?"

Still, they kept silent. Embarrassment burned Nathalie's cheeks.

"Can you stand up?" Barak asked. "Or do you need medical assistance?"

Asaf got up first, lending Nathalie a hand. She winced and put a hand on her back, but the pain felt like a bad bruise.

"I'll be all right," she said.

"Then I have to take you to the police station for interviews. I'll try to make them snappy. I have more important matters to deal with than a couple of amateur sleuths."

Thankfully, the interview was indeed short and snappy. Barak didn't respond when Nathalie said, "I hope this has changed your views about loners," but he did wait a second before continuing.

Eventually, Nathalie signed the statement and made a quick phone call while she waited for Asaf. When he and Barak appeared in the waiting room, Barak said, "I'm letting you two go. But stay around. You might be needed for the trial." He looked at Asaf. "And you'd better learn to talk before then."

Asaf put his arm round Nathalie as they left the building. "Are you sure you're all right?" he asked her, his voice full of concern.

"Well, that was a big shock. And it's still hurting where he dug his knee in."

"I should never have let you go. I should have gone on my own."

"I'm glad we did it together." Anger flashed through Nathalie as she sensed a tendency to want to make decisions for her, but it soon waned and was joined by gratitude. She didn't normally like to be controlled, yet now, after their recent ordeal, she needed someone else to lead for a bit. And when she remembered who Asaf had been for so long, the anger was replaced by admiration for the daring in his chivalry. He was changing and she liked this new assertive Asaf. Or maybe this was the old Asaf, the one that had been covered up for so long. She'd always believed he had been there, hiding.

"Are you sure you don't want to go to hospital to be checked up?" Asaf asked.

"No, it's not that bad. I'm sure it'll heal on its own."

"Then I'll take you home in a taxi. We have a lot to talk about, but first you need to rest."

As they sat side-by-side in the back of the taxi, he took her hand in both of his, and she thought of the beast changing into a prince.

"*Tu es mon prince*," she murmured.

"What does that mean?"

"I'll tell you later." Nathalie lay her head on Asaf's shoulder and he slid his arm behind her back.

Chapter 28: Grandma in the Nettles

"Can I phone you tomorrow?" Asaf asked on emerging from the taxi into the cold, night air. He pulled his hood up, preparing to walk home.

"You can do better than that," said Nathalie. "Come in with me and help me tell our story to the others."

"But it's almost midnight."

"Don't worry. They're waiting for us."

And so they were, ready to provide a heroes' welcome. Both Tehila and Yarden scorned their reluctance to accept the hero status.

"You were so brave," said Yarden. "Stupid but brave,"

"We were this close to death," said Nathalie, holding her thumb and forefinger half a centimetre apart. "And we would have been dead if it hadn't been for Asaf."

"Asaf?" said Yarden and Tehila.

"Me?" said Asaf.

"No doubt of it." The scene came flooding back to Nathalie. "We were lying on the floor, so close we were touching. I felt a hand gripping my neck. Asaf had a knife on his. I was frozen; I couldn't move or speak. But Asaf talked to him and made him answer instead of getting on with the job of… Otherwise we'd have been dead when the police arrived."

Asaf shrugged. "It was intuition, I guess. I felt you there, next to me, shivering from fright. I had to do something to save you, anything to keep you alive. I couldn't move because I was pinned down, so the only thing I could do was to talk. It didn't matter what I said or what anyone would think of it. I had to save you from that murderer."

Nathalie, next to Asaf on the sofa, reached up and planted a kiss on his cheek. "Thank you for saving my life."

Asaf kissed her back and kept his arm around her waist. "Thank you for believing in me."

Tehila touched Yarden and nodded towards the kitchen. They both slipped out to prepare a small feast, leaving the other two alone for a while.

Asaf broke away but remained close. "Really, I mean it. No one ever believed in me before you. And this last business when they all accused me even after I was released – well, I was at my wits' end. I didn't know how I was going to cope with it. But then you came, and you never doubted I was innocent. I needed that so much."

"They all saw you as a beast, but I knew you were a prince."

"And you are Beauty. I remember that movie."

"One day, I'll tell you the real story, but the Disney one will do for now."

Sipping hot chocolate beside the love of her life, munching on a sweet croissant heated from frozen, not perfect but not bad, Nathalie suddenly remembered that other people had lives, too. "Yarden, I'm so sorry. With all this going on, I completely forgot about your project. Did you manage to complete it?"

Yarden sighed. "It's still in a muddle. It feels like random essays rather than a single work that leads from one topic to the next. This is going to be an all-nighter."

"Can I help?" Asaf asked. "Sometimes it can help when someone who doesn't understand the details looks at the whole from above."

"Thanks for offering," said Yarden, "but it's about forensic science. You'd probably find it boring."

“Not at all. In any case, I don’t think I’ll need to spend long at it.”

Yarden explained the project and showed Asaf all the pieces she’d written. Within an hour he’d written a table of contents and organised everything into one large document.

“Look,” he said. “All you have to do now is to write something that connects between these two sections and you’ll be finished.”

“Asaf, you’re amazing. How can I ever thank you for all this?”

“From what I heard, you did plenty for me. This was the least I could do.” Asaf looked around the room. Do you have a printer here?”

“No,” said Yarden. “I can use one at the university in the morning. I’ll have to get there early.”

“Why don’t you come round to my place and I’ll print it for you. Then we can make sure it’s all perfect and you won’t get flustered in the morning.”

“Are you sure? It’s very late.”

“That’s all right,” said Asaf. “It’s not as if I have to go to work tomorrow.”

“I’ve finished,” Yarden called from behind the piles on the floor.

All four went off to Asaf’s flat, making good use of the printer he took out of the *boydem*. By the time they’d finished, dawn was breaking. Yarden and Tehila returned home to catch an hour of sleep and Nathalie stayed to talk. At least, that’s what they said they’d do, but when they found themselves alone, another plan seemed preferable.

Asaf raised his eyebrows. “Are you sure you’re up to it?”

“Don’t worry. I’m feeling much better now.”

“The sofa only opens into a single bed.”

"I think that'll be sufficient," said Nathalie. "The closeness will keep my feet warm, for a change."

"And I do have some condoms. I bought them once, hoping the time would come."

"I think it has."

By the time they woke up, it was getting dark again.

"We missed a whole day," said Nathalie.

"No," said Asaf. "We gained a whole night. It was the most wonderful night I've ever had."

"Mine, too."

They rolled to face each other and embraced.

"Do you mean that?" asked Asaf. "Didn't I act as if I didn't know what to do?"

"Not at all. You were very natural," said Nathalie, adding, "Is it worth getting up or shall we stay in bed?"

"It's tempting to stay here, but I'm feeling a bit peckish."

"Okay. We can eat the rest of the lasagne."

Over the meal, they made plans for the evening. "Let's do something childish and crazy," said Asaf.

"Sounds good. What's it going to be?"

"I know. We can watch a movie and snog in the back row."

"You don't think we might be doing things in the wrong order?"

"Yes, but who cares?"

"Okay, let's go for it."

In the cinema, sitting at the back, they shared out the popcorn equally, half for Asaf and half for Nathalie. And they giggled. And snogged.

"This is like going back to adolescence," said Nathalie.

"This is better than adolescence," said Asaf.

"Why?"

"Childhood is full of restrictions. But as adults, we can do what we like."

"Shh," said a few people around them.

"I guess I was wrong," whispered Asaf.

The whispering made Nathalie's ear tingle. She found that exceedingly pleasant.

After the film, they decided to spend the night together in Nathalie's place. Nathalie needed some clean clothes, and Tehila and Yarden were eager for gossip.

"How are the lovebirds?" asked Tehila, her eyes twinkling.

"The lovebirds are tweeting from the treetops," said Asaf.

"What have I missed here?" Nathalie asked.

"You'll be pleased to hear that I dumped Tom," said Tehila.

"Well done," said Nathalie. "There are plenty more fish in the sea, even for someone as ugly as you."

"Hey, watch it."

"I gave in my project on time, thanks to you two," said Yarden.

Nathalie invited Asaf into her room while she busied herself with clothes, picking out warm trousers and a favourite multi-coloured sweater that she would take to the bathroom for a quick shower.

She laid the clothes on the bed and Asaf gave an admiring murmur. "You always look smart and special."

Nathalie smiled. "I like to choose clothes that impress. It's part of being French, I suppose."

"It's part of being you. I like your room, too. It's really tidy and cosy in here." Asaf sounded surprised.

"Unlike the rest of the apartment, you mean."

Asaf grinned.

"You're right. The others have become very good friends and I don't like to complain too much, but the state of this place gets me down, sometimes."

Nathalie picked out a book from a shelf. “We’re going to read this together,” she said.

“But it’s in French.”

“I’ll translate,” said Nathalie.

Asaf read from the cover. “*La Belle et la Bête*. The beauty and the… Is this *Beauty and the Beast*?”

“It is.”

“*Hayafa vehachaya*. Great story.”

“This is the original story, written by a woman called Gabrielle-Suzanne Barbot de Villeneuve in 1740, long before Disney existed. It’s an important story – and it’s ours. I want you to love it as I do.”

“I’ll do my best.”

“We need to create the right atmosphere to read it. Something that fits the time and place where it was written.”

“Ooh, that sounds fun. Eighteenth century. I’m surprised a woman wrote it.”

“When you have money, you can do what you like. On the other hand, when you don’t have money, you’re forced to act to get some. Madame de Villeneuve grew up with money, but her husband lost a lot of it before she divorced him, and then she lost a lot more.”

“What a mine of information you are.”

“Only about French literature.” Nathalie leafed through the pages of the book. “Look, here’s a picture of the author.”

“She looks very sedate, sitting upright on that chair.”

“She’s posing for a portrait. What do you expect? She probably had to sit for hours in that position.”

“She’s wearing a long, flowing, cream-coloured dress with russet-coloured flowers. The beads on her necklace are the same sort of colour and the bow on her sleeve is, too. Also, the material of the chair she’s sitting on, with the curved legs. And the bow in her hair. I love the way it all matches.”

Nathalie drew up a chair to search in a high cupboard. “We’re not going to get it completely right, but it’ll be enough to imagine. Look, here’s a sheet with a flowery pattern. I’ll drape it round me. And Tehila might have a necklace like that.”

“She’s also wearing white gloves and her sleeve has an enormous cuff.”

“*Il ne faut pas pousser mémé dans les orties!*”

“What on earth does that mean?”

“It means: One shouldn’t push Grandma in the nettles.”

Asaf burst out laughing, which, for Nathalie, was a first. She might have looked surprised.

“Sorry, I couldn’t help imagining Grandma in the nettles.”

“It’s an expression.”

“So I gathered.”

“It means: No need to exaggerate.”

“I see. Nothing like the grandma expression in Hebrew, then.”

“What’s that?”

“When someone tells you a story you don’t believe, you could say, ‘Tell it to your grandma,’ meaning: I don’t believe a word you said, but you might have better luck with your grandma.”

Nathalie grinned. “That’s a good one to remember.”

“We’ll have to exchange more expressions, sometime. What will I wear?”

“Eh?”

“What will I wear for this evening’s performance?”

Nathalie jumped down from the chair and turned the page. “Here’s a picture of Madame de Villeneuve’s partner at the time. He’s called Prosper Jolyot de Crébillon.”

“I hope there won’t be a test at the end. I’ve forgotten that name, already. I see he has a brown cloak that’s pinned at the top of his shoulder. It looks like a blanket.”

“Good idea. I have a brown blanket.” She opened up the blanket that had been folded at the end of her bed and draped it over Asaf, using safety pins on his shoulders to keep the folds in place. Then she stepped back. "Perfect."

With Tehila's help, the chair was covered with dark orange material and Nathalie's hair was tied up and decorated with a dark orange brooch.

In the end, Tehila and Yarden watched the performance, too. They formed the audience, while Asaf was given pride of place in the front row, facing Nathalie.

With the help of pictures from the book, Nathalie told the whole story. Parts of it were pretty gruesome, others sweet and loving. The ending was deliciously sweet, linking Beauty's belief in the Beast with his transformation into a handsome prince.

When Nathalie finished, Asaf stood up and pulled Nathalie up to embrace her, amid wild applause from the other two. All four had tears in their eyes.

A few days later, the couple had seesawed back to Asaf's place. They'd cashed in on their joint love of walking and had used the opportunity provided by the temporary closure of their office and the sunny weather to explore some local outdoor sites. The Haas Promenade welcomed them back. They also walked along the Mesila Park, in one direction to the First Station cultural and culinary centre, and in the other to the Biblical Zoo, which they entered and explored.

"Wow, another hill," said Nathalie. The midday winter sun was beating down in the way she'd expected it to do every day, before moving to Jerusalem. It pleased Nathalie but also made climbing tough.

"Have I made you walk too much?" Worry seeped into Asaf's voice and countenance.

"No, not at all. But I will have a rest when we reach the top. I can see a bench up there."

When they walked to the First Station, they continued into Yemin Moshe and Nathalie pointed out Carmel's house. She also remembered her question.

"Is there a song about Moses Montefiore?"

"Yes. In the song, the angels keep coming to tell him his time is up, but he tells them he can't go yet because there are still people he needs to help. Then he gets up on his carriage and off he goes."

"How sweet."

One evening, having managed to obtain last minute tickets, they watched a play, a comedy that was also thought-provoking. Nathalie found that, after studying the description of the play so that she knew what to expect, it wasn't hard at all to follow.

She was thrilled at the end. "I worried I wasn't going to be able to understand anything. But I did understand most of it and your whispered explanations helped with the rest."

He squeezed her hand and she squeezed back.

"It was probably the simple language of that play. I'm sure I wouldn't understand most plays."

"Hey, what was that you told me about believing in yourself?"

Both knew this time together, blocking out the rest of the world, couldn't go on for ever, but neither wanted to think about the future, yet.

"Nathalie…"

She turned to look at him, catching the intensity written on his face.

"You won't ever leave me, will you?"

"No, I won't ever leave you."

"Then, could I ask you something?"

Chapter 29: Locked Up

Prison was a dreadful place. But he would survive it because he deserved to be there. He had committed the ultimate crime – he'd taken away a life, and for that he deserved all the punishment he received.

And really, his own life had not been good before that. Not good at all. He looked around the cell, at the bed, the mattress, the bedding, even the clothes he was wearing. None of them belonged to him. Yet, he didn't miss any of his own things. Apart from one. And while he couldn't touch that one thing, he could see it, every night, and talk to it. As soon as he closed his eyes, it came to him, lying in the open drawer. The plastic box and inside it, the heart-shaped brooch.

"Iris, please, I beg of you, talk to me."

"Hello, Eran."

He couldn't believe it. Finally, after all this time. "Iris, is that really you?"

"Yes, it's me."

The voice echoed, but he was sure it was hers.

"How come you're talking to me here in this awful place and after I did the worst thing I could do, and yet you never talked to me at home when you could have helped me."

"Because…because I couldn't have helped you. I didn't deserve to help you."

"What do you mean?"

"I'm going to tell you a secret, something you mustn't tell a soul."

"Ha." His laughter was mocking and bitter. "Who could I tell in this terrible place?"

"Eran, I wasn't the perfect person you thought I was. You were so much in love with me that you didn't realise. I had all sorts of flaws. The main one was that I used to steal things. I didn't need the things I stole, but I couldn't help myself. There was a purple pen, a silky scarf that would never have stayed on my head, a shoe – yes, just one shoe. Remember, you'd ask where something came from and I'd make some excuse? I stole it. Now do you see? I was a thief and a liar. I was a bad person, through and through, and I didn't deserve to live. That's why I didn't fight for my health when I got ill. I remained passive and let the disease attack me from within. I knew my fate: the disease would end in death.

"What you have to do now is to wake up to the truth. Serve your sentence, whatever it is, and then enjoy the rest of your life and don't ever think of me again, except as a bad person who caused you no end of trouble. Goodbye, Eran."

Eran heard the voice fading away, leaving him.

"Iris, come back," he called.

But she didn't return, and Eran knew his cries were futile. Over the next few days, he shed more tears than he had in his whole life up to then.

Chapter 30: Party Time

Asaf surveyed the room. It looked much bigger without all the clutter. Even Yarden had managed to clear away all her stuff and store it in her bedroom, or rather, to toss it in. Little snacks had been placed around the room. The larger dishes and drinks had been laid out on the dining table, where peonies peering out of a beige vase lent their pink and purple colours to the scene. He still had to keep reminding himself this was reality. Self-belief still didn't come naturally, but he was getting there.

He'd done his bit in helping to prepare, but now the kitchen didn't need his presence. It was full enough with three excited girls working to put the final touches to the dishes.

The doorbell rang and Asaf rushed to open it. His mother reached up to give him warm hug.

"Darling, I'm so happy for you."

His father's hug was less tight, more manly, but with a pat on the back. Clearly, he was happy, too.

Asaf laid their coats on Nathalie's bed and returned to them. Three smiling faces appeared from the kitchen.

"Which one of these lovely girls is Nathalie?"

Asaf kept watching his mother's smiling face, seeing the fear that seasoned the excitement. *She's worried it'll turn out to be Tehila.* He grinned. *Let her worry for a moment.*

Then Nathalie stepped forwards and introduced herself. Asaf's mother took in the dress, smart but not showy, above the knee but not too short. She noted high-heeled, silver shoes and natural long brown hair hanging loose, the front strands tied back with a red bow. The make-up on the sweet face was not overdone. Eventually, his mother gave a nod of approval.

Then she said, "How does it feel to be marrying a loner?"

Nathalie's eyes opened wide.

Seeing Nathalie's reaction, his mother added, "Don't worry. I know it's all rubbish. I don't know where they got that 'loner' thing from. And then instead of apologising for their mistake, they went on to publish a whole article about loners as if it had come from our Asaf. You know, I used to think there was some truth in newspaper articles but now I know they're all made up."

The smiles that passed between Asaf and Nathalie brimmed with meaning that was lost to his mother.

Next to arrive were Barak and Shira, whooping their congratulations before handing over their coats and a bottle of wine. Barak looked ten years younger.

"I don't think I need to ask whether you're enjoying retirement," said Nathalie.

Barak squeezed his wife. "*We* are enjoying it very much."

"What about that holiday you missed because of me?" asked Asaf.

"In Eilat? We're going next week. And nothing's going to stop us this time. Not even you." He pointed an accusing finger at Asaf, but his face told a different story.

A shout of *mazal tov* erupted as all the office people arrived together.

"You beat us to it," said Sagi, her arm around Kfir. "You'll come to our celebration next week, won't you?"

"We're looking forward to it," said Asaf.

Gidon gave Barak a slap on the back. "Braki!"

"Gidi!"

"Do you two know each other?"

"We're cousins," said Gidon.

"Practically grew up together," said Barak.

“Hmm,” said Nathalie, suddenly recalling Gidon’s phone call, urging her to stop investigating. This development put it in a new light.

Three more people arrived: Aviva, Hila and the baby. Everyone gathered around the infant, cooing at him.

“What’s his name?” Nathalie asked.

“Asaf. It’s my tribute to a man who suffered because of a vile liar who fooled me for a while.”

“Thank you,” said Asaf. “It’s true I suffered, but the events that followed that unfortunate incident have more than made up for that.” He squeezed Nathalie to prove it.

“I’m so sorry all this happened to you,” Nathalie said to Hila.

“Oh, I think it was all for the best in the end. I have to say, you played the part of private investigator very well. You seemed professional, but you were also really kind to me at that terrible time.”

Nathalie blushed. “Thank you. I felt bad about deceiving you like that.”

“Not at all. I’m glad you came and told me the truth about Ido. Do you know I’ve been in contact with Ido’s former wives?”

“No. Were they friendly?”

“They’re very friendly. And they’re both going to come to visit soon with their children. After all, they’re little Asaf’s half brothers and sisters.”

Gidon took big Asaf to one side. “I want to apologise on several accounts. I never understood you before. If I’d known you better, I would never have suspected you of murder, of course. I’ve only recently discovered how important you were in the team. We’re all missing you and struggling without you. If you wanted to come back, I’d make sure you were well rewarded.”

“That’s very nice of you,” said Asaf, “but after everything that happened, I feel it’s time for me to move on and start afresh. I want to work in an office where no one knows me. I want to see if I can rise to the challenge of being…normal. As it happens, I just found a new job and agreed to start next week."

"I understand completely. Our loss is their gain. I wish you lots of success in your new life."

"I also have something to celebrate," Yarden announced to the crowd. "I only heard today. I got 96 for my project. The lecturer wrote, 'Excellent content and organisation.' I didn't mention that a certain famous electronics engineer helped with the organisation, but I can't thank him enough."

"That's all right," said Asaf. "A certain clever criminology student helped a lot to get a famous electronics engineer out of jail."

At that point, Asaf suddenly noticed Zahava lurking in the corner, her lips tucked in between her teeth and eyes lowered. "Zahava, I didn't see you before."

She came forward. "Congratulations, Asaf and Nathalie. To tell you the truth, I was surprised to be invited after the way I treated you when you'd just been released."

"Oh, don't worry. I don't bear any grudges. It was a difficult situation."

"Well, that's very kind of you."

Arik, who had entered with the office crowd, cornered Nathalie. She felt shocked for a moment, but comforted by the surrounding crowds. Had they really invited him? Then she remembered they'd sent a general invitation to the whole office. She hadn't even considered that he might come, as he only appeared once a month.

"Don't worry," said Arik. "I wanted to apologise for my behaviour in the restaurant. I was feeling anxious and vulnerable, but my behaviour was reprehensible. I'm so sorry."

Nathalie nodded. "I can't say I wasn't scared out of my wits on that day. I saw fury written on your face, and in your voice. I was shivering from fright."

"You have every reason to hate me, but I hope you'll be able to forgive me, partly."

Nathalie wondered. Maybe, over time, forgiveness was possible.

"I hate myself for what I caused you, but it made me come to a decision. I admitted everything to my wife, and she understood and forgave me. Now, I'm studying to get that qualification."

Nathalie smiled. "I'm so glad it worked out for you."

"Nathalie, there you are," said Omer, coming over. "Am I interrupting anything?"

"Not at all," said Arik. "She's all yours."

Omer bent down to Nathalie's level. His surprise came as a whisper. "Don't tell this to anyone yet, but we're going to have to look for a new systems manager."

"Oh, has Charlie left?"

"In a way. Charlie has been…detained, and will remain so for a very long time."

"Wow. How do you know that, if the news hasn't been published yet?"

"Let's say I heard it through the grapevine."

Nathalie opened her eyes wide and Omer added, "You're at liberty to believe or not believe anything you hear, but I request that you don't discuss this with anyone, yet. I'm telling you because I'm sure you must have suspected him anyway, while you were investigating."

Omer vanished into the crowd, leaving Nathalie to remember her suspicions about him. He wasn't the murderer, as she'd once thought, but he also wasn't completely open. Secrets definitely lurked in his head.

"Has everyone seen the latest about the murder?" asked Asaf, holding up a newspaper and surprising himself with the loudness of his voice.

Most of those present had seen it, but Asaf's parents skimmed through.

"So the murderer, Eran, grappled the knife from Ido's hand."

"But the knife was there in his hand. Ido was ready to use it on Eran. Can you believe it?"

No one could really swallow all they'd heard about Ido, but they were beginning to accept that it must be true.

"Could I say something?" No one recognised the youngish man who stepped forward, but Asaf guessed who he was. He had the advantage of having been asked if this person could come, if he was able to muster the courage. Apparently, Barak came from a large family, to which this man's wife slotted in, somehow.

The room became strangely quiet. "I'm really sorry to be a party pooper," he began, "but it's important to me to explain something to the people involved in this unfortunate incident…murder. My name is Guy. I'm Eran's younger brother. Growing up, we were very close. Eran always looked after me and protected me. I owe so much to him. Then we grew up and married. We didn't see quite as much of each other, but we remained just as close. Eran adored his wife, Iris. They never had children. It was just the two of them, and they did everything together. It was a perfect, loving relationship that was heart-warming to behold from the outside, but it was that perfection that caused my brother's downfall.

"When Iris became ill, Eran cared for her, night and day. Still, the inevitable happened and he was left alone. He couldn't cope with it. He should have sought professional help. As a psychologist himself, he thought he had all the answers and didn't need help from anyone. Instead, he became a substance user and abuser; he lost his job and he attempted suicide. The rest you know. I bear a huge weight of guilt that I didn't do more for him. Despite everything, I still love my brother and hate to think of him languishing in jail. I know that will only add to his suffering.

"That's all. I felt I owed you an explanation, and I hope you understand him better now."

As he made for the exit, Nathalie said, "Won't you stay and have some refreshments?"

"No, thank you. You'll enjoy your party better without me. Congratulations."

Conversations were indeed muted following Guy's departure until Tehila decided it was time for the video. She turned on the TV and everyone crowded around it to watch.

When it began, Nathalie called out, "*Maman*!" and she and Asaf were pushed to the front. No one but Nathalie understood the words, but the general meaning was clear. The members of her family appeared, one by one, to congratulate her and Asaf, and wish them all the best for the future.

"They promised to come for the wedding," a beaming Nathalie said when it was over. "My sister said we mustn't get married in August, because of the baby."

"Your mother will be able to meet mine," said Asaf. "They'll be able to gossip together."

"But they don't speak the same language."

"I don't think a minor problem like that will get in their way." Asaf winked.

Then someone turned some lively music on, and Barak and Shira started to dance. Others held on to them and joined in, and in no time, there was a long line of dancers snaking around the room. Even Zahava forgot previous worries and started to enjoy the moment. The wine, the food, the music and the company had done their job of lightening the mood in the room.

On her way out, Reut, who'd had a few drinks, said to Asaf, "You know, you're quite a handsome bloke for a loner."

Asaf took a step back from the mini-skirted, lipstick-smudged flirt. "Reut," he said, "I'm taken and so are you."

"Oh yes," said Reut, turning down the corners of her lips.

"Come on, Reut," said Gidon. "Time to go home to your poor husband and kids."

Finally, Asaf and Nathalie were alone, having been banned from helping in the kitchen. They lay entwined on the sofa.

"That went well, didn't it?" said Asaf.

"It went brilliantly," said Nathalie, her head nestled in Asaf's embrace. "Couldn't have been better." Then she added, "You are talking about the party, aren't you?"

"Yes. What else could I be talking about?"

"Solving the crime. That went well, too."

"Yes and no. We were lucky the police arrived when they did."

"That's true. But the main thing is that we discovered we work well as a team and not just in a work environment."

"'We work well as a team.' I never thought I'd hear anyone say that about me."

"But it's true, don't you think?"

"Yes, although I don't expect we'll ever have to solve a murder again."

"Ooh, you never know."

Asaf gave Nathalie a squeeze. "So, tell me: how does it feel to be engaged to a beast?"

"I'm not engaged to a beast. I'm engaged to a handsome prince, and it feels like a fairy tale."

THE END

Thank you for reading my book. I hope you enjoyed the story; that was my main reason for writing it. If you also learned something from it, that would be an added advantage. If you liked the book, please take a moment to leave a review for it at your favourite retailer.

If you want to find out more about social anxiety, please consider my non-fiction book: *Social Anxiety Revealed.* And do look out for more novels in this series.

Thanks!
Miriam Drori

Ocelot Press

Thank you for reading this novel released through **Ocelot Press**. If you enjoyed it, we'd greatly appreciate it if you could take a moment to write a short review on the website where you bought the book, and/or on Goodreads, and recommend it to a friend. Sharing your thoughts helps other readers to choose good books and authors to keep writing.

You might like to try books by other **Ocelot Press** authors. We cover a range of genres, with a focus on historical fiction (including historical mystery and paranormal), romance, fantasy and now crime fiction. To find out more, please don't hesitate to connect with us on:

Website: **https://ocelot-press.com**
Twitter: **www.twitter.com/OcelotPress**
Facebook: **www.facebook.com/OcelotPress**

Printed in Great Britain
by Amazon

11512754R00119